THE FREDRIC BROWN PULP DETECTIVE SERIES

And, ..., more to come!

The **Fredric Brown Pulp Detective Series** presents the best of his previously uncollected work, plus some previously unpublished material, primarily in the mystery genre, but also including some sf and fantasy pieces.

THE FREAK SHOW MURDERS

Fredric Brown
in the
Detective Pulps
VOL. 5

1985

Cover design by William L. McMillan

First paperback edition published December 1986

Dennis McMillan Publications
1995 Calais Dr. No. 3
Miami Beach, FL 33141

TABLE OF CONTENTS

NICE MYSTERIES
Richard A. Lupoff

Last Saturday I drove into the city and squeezed into a parking place around the corner from Bruce Taylor's shop. Taylor runs the San Francisco Mystery Bookstore.

It's a tiny store, crammed with a gorgeous jumble of breath-taking collectables and tattered reading copies. A while after I arrived I was invisible, burrowed into a cranny searching for a lost treasure. Like the proverbial fly-on-the-wall I could peer out and observe and overhear a conversation without the speakers noticing that I was there.

Two archetypal little-old-ladies were giving Taylor their joint want-list. Taylor was telling them about his experience meeting a popular mystery writer whose private eye often uses marijuana and other marginally illegal relaxants.

"That's terrible," one of the little-old-ladies scolded. "I certainly wouldn't want to read about that, and I can't imagine why anyone would want to write about it."

"But it goes on all the time," Taylor said gently. Taylor is a huge man with a fierce black moustache. He looks a lot like Robert B. Parker. Like many such brawny types, he has developed a startlingly gentle manner of speech and movement.

"It's in the newspaper every day," he said. "Why shouldn't authors write about it? Why do you object to reading about it?"

"Because," the second little-old-lady asserted through pursed lips, "we like to read *nice* books about *nice* mysteries!"

* * * *

They didn't go into detail as to what "nice mysteries" are, but then there was really no need. The two little-old-ladies were talking about the kind of genteel, traditionally English, tea-with-the-vicar mystery novels associated with Agatha Christie, Doris Miles Disney, Georgette Heyer, and their whole school, down to P.D. James and Marion Babson.

But this is fantasy.

It is as much fantasy as are the works of Tolkien and T.H. White, Marion Zimmer Bradley and Katherine Kurtz and Piers Anthony. A different *kind* of fantasy, but these *nice* mysteries have as little connection with real crime and detection as tales of unicorns and trolls and wizards and fairies (or "faeries") have to do with real life and struggle and death.

Chandler said it first and best, of course, writing about a contemporary: "Hammett took murder out of the Venetian vase and dropped it into the alley . . . Hammett gave murder back to the kind of people that commit it for reasons, not just to provide a corpse; and with the means at hand, not with handwrought duelling pistols, curare, and tropical fish."

The pulp tradition of mystery writing falls somewhere between that grim and brutal reality, and the genteel fantasy of tea-with-the-vicar.

(And, aside, is it not puzzling that little-old-ladies *want* murder to take place in their genteel fantasies? I will not offer my theory as to why this is so, although I have one.)

The pulp story in general and the pulp mystery in particular represent a distinct approach to writing, with definite standards and requirements. Subtlety was a vice, characterization was performed with broad fast swipes of strong pigment, *plot* was rudimentary in the sense that complex relationships or moral ambiguities were eschewed in favor of white hats battling black hats, but *story* was all-important in terms of the requirement that things kept happening all the time.

The ideal was to grab the reader by the nose in paragraph one and start running at top speed and never let up until you had reached the end.

The very best writers outgrew the pulps. Hammett and Chandler of course and also John D. MacDonald and Cornell Woolrich and Horace McCoy, and if better researchers than I are to be believed, Stephen Crane and Jack London and Upton Sinclair and Mackinlay Kantor and Sinclair Lewis and Ray Bradbury. Whether their stories continued to appear in pulp magazines or not, they had triumphed over the form.

And the worst pulp writers—well, citing Mickey Spillane is like shooting fish in a barrel. What does Mick care, he doesn't even have to laugh all the way to the bank any more. They send a bonded messenger in an armored truck to make Mick's pickups.

Fredric Brown went to neither of these extremes. He did not transcend the pulp form, but neither did he pander to it or to the baser instincts of his readers. Within the limits of the established pulp form he worked with high competence and responsibility. He gave his editors and his readers honest value for value tendered. He was an honest story-teller, he respected the traditions and the formulas of the fields in which he worked. Yet he brought a pleasant tincture of originality to many of his stories. He mixed a touch of the macabre with a dash of sardonic humor.

8

The result was a menu of essentially standard dishes, yet each served with a distinctive and often elusive flare that was Fred Brown's own trademark.

This we find in his mysteries, his science fiction stories, and in his occasional forays into other realms.

In 1956 Brown contributed an essay titled "Where Do You Get Your Plot?" to Herbert Brean's compilation, *The Mystery Writer's Handbook.* Brown claimed that all writers constructed their stories the same way; it was just that some of them did it on a subconscious level while others did it consciously. Brown wrote this:

"A writer plots by accretion. If you've forgotten what the word means I'll save you a trip to the dictionary—it means *increase by gradual addition.*

"It can start with anything—a character, a theme, a setting, a single word. By accretion it builds or is built into a plot."

In his essay Brown goes on to construct a story from a single word, "goldfish." Although he doesn't say so in "Where Do You Get Your Plot?" the goldfish story was apparently one that he had written several years earlier. In somewhat transmogrified form it seemingly became (had become) "A Cat Walks" in *Detective Story Magazine* in 1942.

Locale was important in many pulp stories, immaterial or even anonymous in others. This of course is equally true outside of the pulps. Stories of show biz centered on Broadway or Hollywood for obvious reasons, although in at least one yarn Brown used a "little theatre" background that could be set in any city. Writers of high adventure clung to the glamorous and mysterious trappings of Tibet, Yucatan, or Cairo.

In the detection field, at least until Chandler added Los Angeles to the list, most stories took place in London, San Francisco, New York, Paris, or Chicago. I suppose Paris appears on the list because so many of the para-fictional crime memoirs of the nineteenth century took place there, as did the immortal Poe's stories of the Chevalier Dupin.

Doyle deserves credit for London's popularity, I suppose, but he has to share that with Dickens and Collins and the wonderful shrouding fog. And that fog, I think, is a major reason for the laying of so many tales in San Francisco.

But New York and Chicago were the gang capitals of the nation during the heyday of the pulps, and the placing of gangster stories there was as natural in that day as is the flashing of spy-thrillers between Washington and Moscow today.

The stories in the present volume don't rely heavily on Chicago settings even though Fred Brown was an old Chicago boy himself. The major yarn, "The Freak Show Murders," has as its background an itinerant carnival; although various towns are visited in the course of the story, it's the carnival itself that is the real setting for the tale.

The killings themselves are somewhat bizarre. They come close to "the Venetian vase . . . handwrought duelling pistols, curare, and tropical fish." But there is nothing here of the genteel vicarage school of writing. "The Freak Show Murders" is, in at least one scene, chillingly anticipatory of Graham Greene's "The Third Man." And in overall tone, "The Freak Show Murders" resonates with William Lindsay Gresham's jolting and unforgettable *Nightmare Alley* — which it predates by three years.

Brown had other strings on his bow.

"Double Murder" (published under the pseudonym John S. Endicott) features one of the neatest bits of misdirection you'll come across in a library full of mysteries.

And "Two Biers for Two," a tough gangster story of the classic style, features one of the most powerful — and bloody — images you're likely to encounter this year. It also includes some neat and unexpected foreshadowing. The reader gets that little surge of pleasure that comes when all the pieces slip neatly into place.

Memorable characters are not numerous in these stories, for two reasons which converge to prevent their growth.

One is the nature of pulp writing. James Blish said that pulp characters typically possessed only those characteristics needed to function in their roles in the story. A ship's captain in a pulp story (starship captain in a science fiction story, steamship captain in a modern romance, pirate captain in a swashbuckler) had only those elements required to play his part. Intelligence, courage, technical and tactical knowledge.

But in a well-executed literary work, that captain would have a childhood and education behind him, a chosen flavor of ice cream, a religious preference, and very likely a favorite poet, baseball team, and brand of beer.

Blish's notion wasn't altogether invalid, but it also wasn't altogether fair.

The problem of the short story versus that of the novel must also be considered. Philip K. Dick said that the short story was about things that people did while the novel was about people who did things.

There just isn't that much room in a short story, to develop character. That's true as a generality in both pulp and literary short stories, but it is intensified and re-intensified in the pulp short story with its requirement for constant action.

Fred Brown's characters aren't really badly drawn, they're just a trifle too sketchy. I find myself wanting to know Mortimer Tracy better—and George Hearn of the Springfield police department as he tries to figure out if the murderer was a rooster wearing silk pajamas—and private eye Carey Rix.

When Brown did stretch out more, as in "The Freak Show Murders," he *did* develop his characters more. We learn, at least, that carnival barker Pete Gaynor is 36 years old, was passed over by the World War II draft board because he has just a touch of hemophilia, and wants very much to marry beautiful Stella the snake girl.

Pulp writers got around the problem of undercharacterization in their short stories by writing series about the same people. Readers liked that because they became fond of the characters and wanted to see them return. Editors liked it because that boosted sales. And authors liked it because it tended to provide some stability in a terrifyingly unreliable marketplace. It also saved them the trouble of dreaming up a whole new cast of characters every time they set out to do a new story.

Thus there were Carroll John Daly's Race Williams, Robert E. Howard's Breckinridge Elkins, Johnston McCulley's Zorro, and of course Hammett's immortal Continental Op.

Fred Brown had Ed and Am Hunter, an uncle-nephew private eye team. Their adventures filled volumes.

But the stories in *this* book rest not on character but on Brown's wry and ingenious way of constructing and then revealing the structure of his crimes and their solutions. While far from the grim and violent stories we have learned to expect from some of our more modern practitioners, Brown's stories still have at the heart that ultimate crime murder.

I'm sure that those two little old ladies twittering away at poor gentle Bruce Taylor would not care for this book. They would not consider Fredric Brown's crime stories, *nice* mysteries.

But the trouble, damn it all, is that crime is seldom nice and murder is *never* nice.

Say, has anybody used that yet as a title?

Richard A. Lupoff
Berkeley, California
February, 1985

DOUBLE MURDER

Chapter I: Bolt of a Nut

The tall man in the poorly fitting gray suit looked about cautiously before he stepped out of the doorway. Down the long vista of street lights glimmering in the twilight haze, only a few pedestrians were visible. And none of them were near except the fellow who had obviously been celebrating too enthusiastically.

The tall man's knees shook just a little as he stepped out into the open of the sidewalk. He felt the strength of steel springs in his muscles, but his hands felt naked. Empty. Without a knife.

A cold wind blew along the street, blew up the open cuffs of trousers that were a good three inches too short for him. Trousers that obviously had been made to fit a shorter and heavier man. Up the thin legs of the tall man blew the wind, and it seemed to blow up along his spine, and he shivered.

His somber eyes watched the celebrant, now only a few steps away. The fellow was a big man, with a thick bull-like neck. The tall man's fingers flexed. It would be easy . . . But, no, that way was not fast enough.

People would come running. Policemen. Guards. And they would take him back.

No. He thrust his hands into his pockets, telling himself that he must wait. He must use the cleverness that had enabled him to change — within the few hours since his escape — his uniform suit for the suit he now wore, less conspicuous despite its poor fit.

And the man he had his eyes on had broad shoulders, too. He would put up a fight.

"Say, Mister," the tall man whined, "can you spare something for a guy who ain't eaten in — in days? Just some change, Mister. Honest, I —"

The other man had stopped. He stood there, swaying slightly, his eyes owlish. He lifted a hand and solemnly waggled a thick finger at the suppliant.

"Can't fool me," he said. "Can't fool Tracy. You want money buy drinks, not eats. Drinks. You're bum."

"Huh-uh, Mister. That ain't it. Honest —"

" 'S good idea, drinks. C'mon, I'll buy drinks. Your hat don't fit."

"I don't want —" The tall man broke off abruptly, and his eyes grew crafty. "Sure, Mister. That's swell. But — uh — some quiet place, huh? The way I'm dressed and all —"

The owl-eyed man who called himself Tracy ponderously hooked an arm in the elbow of the man with the ill-fitting clothes.

"Sure. Quiet place. C'mon, pal, we'll go see Joe. Say, 'at rhymes swell. 'Go — Joe —' "

From time to time the tall man surreptitiously pulled at the sleeves of the gray coat to try to make them cover more of his bony wrists, to make himself less conspicuous. He pulled, too, at the brim of the too-tight hat, jamming it tightly down over his forehead. If it fit so badly that even this half-seas-over guy would notice —

He thrust his hands back into his pockets. They felt less naked there. "Gee, thanks, Mister," he said. "I dunno how I can ever —"

"Here's Joe's," said his chance companion, and piloted the tall man through a doorway into a tavern.

Behind the bar was a man even bigger than the celebrant, with a head as bald as the knob of a bannister-post. Otherwise, the place was deserted; too early for the evening crowd.

The man in the ill-fitting clothes sighed audibly with relief. No other customers — what a break. Somewhere they would have —

"Hi, Tracy," said the bald barman. "Third time today. Going in circles around the block?"

Tracy grinned. "Give us a drink, Joe. Give my friend whatever he wants. Mine same as usual. Y'know, Joe, you got something there, about going in circles. Read man's got one leg shorter'n the other. Everybody. Makes you walk in circles. Like pinwheels maybe. Or —"

He talked on and on. The man in the ill-fitting clothes didn't like the way Joe was looking at him. He stepped quickly in closer to the bar and sat down on a stool, his hands out of sight in his lap. That kept his wrists and ankles from the bald man's suspicious stare.

But the bartender didn't keep on looking at him. He put a shot-glass on the bar and filled it from the Golden Eagle bottle, and shoved it across to Tracy, without a chaser.

Then he looked coldly at the slender man.

"Well, bum?" he asked.

The man in the poorly-fitting clothes felt relief. If he was passing for an ordinary moocher, he had cleared the first hurdle. "I — a beer, I guess," he said. "But could I get something to eat first? I — uh —"

"Give him anything he wants, Joe," said Tracy magnanimously. "Maybe the guy *is* hungry. I thought he just had a thirst. Someday,

maybe I'll be where he is, Joe. Maybe you will. Never can tell."
He picked up his glass and downed its contents. "That's why I
never turn a guy down, Joe, when I'm off duty."

Luckily for the tall man, the bartender had been looking at
Tracy and Tracy had been looking at nothing. Neither of them
saw the tall man start suddenly.

"Off duty?" he said. "Are you —"

"Sure, pal, I'm a detective. But don't let it worry you. I got
three days off and I'm celebrating. Panhandling ain't my detail,
annahoo. Now, Joe, you give this here guy whatever he wants.
I'm paying for it, see?"

"Okay, Tracy, okay. I'll take care of him."

The big bartender tapped the slender man on the shoulder.

"Come on, bum. I'll give you some grub in the back room
and leave you there to eat it. Then you scram, see? You don't
look — well, you eat and then scram."

The tall man nodded, and followed the bartender into the back
room. There was a kitchen table there, and chairs around it. The
bartender put a plate of bread on the table, a smaller plate with
some sliced sausage beside it. He turned toward the ice-box in
one corner, then reconsidered.

"That'll do you," he said. "Go ahead."

"Gee, thanks. That's swell."

The tall man sat down at the table and reached for a slice
of bread. Then he froze in that position, motionless, as the bartender turned away and went back to the front room again.

He dropped the bread back on the plate, and pushed the chair
back quietly so it wouldn't scrape. His eyes searched the kitchen
eagerly. There would be a knife somewhere, surely. Where?

His breath was coming fast now, with the nearness of it.

The ice-box? Not so likely. The cupboard? Then, as he stood
up, he saw the drawer of the table at which he had been sitting.
His somber eyes lighted.

With infinite caution, half an inch at a time, he slid the drawer open. It was there!

His whole body trembled — not with fear — as he reached into the drawer and picked up the knife. His hand closed around the hilt of it, and his hand was no longer naked. . . .

Back in the barroom the world revolved around Tracy in pink and black circles. The pink circles were the present, and the black circles were the future.

Oh, not that there was anything violently wrong about the future, past tomorrow morning. But tomorrow morning he would have a hangover, and it would be a dilly. Tracy knew that, though Trace didn't drink often.

This was the first celebration he'd had since — well, since years ago.

Here he had a rare three days off, and because he had done all his celebrating the first day, the second and third days were going to be misery. Anyway, the second.

Something was pounding at his ears. The radio back of the bar. Where was Joe? Oh, yes. He swiveled around on the stool and yelled at the kitchen door:

"Hey, Joe, how's about shutting off this blinkin' yell-box?"

He got up off the stool to go around and shut it off himself, but decided it was too much trouble. Pretty soon he'd better take a taxi home and go to sleep.

That voice on the radio — it sounded exactly like old Cap Molenauer who used to handle the radio car broadcast when he, Tracy, used to be in a radio flivver. But Cap Molenauer was dead now. The alky gang, they thought, had rubbed him out. But they had never proved who did it, and Cap Molenauer had been a swell guy, too.

Tracy cursed the alky gang, then cursed the radio. He gripped the glass that had held the Golden Eagle and wondered if he could throw it straight enough to put the radio out of commission. But he was a force of law and order, on duty or off. He couldn't go throwing glassware around taverns.

"And now for the local news," went on Cap Molenauer, only Cap Molenauer was dead so this must be someone else who had a voice like Cap's. "Carl Lambert, the homicidal maniac who escaped late this afternoon from Belleview Asylum, is still at large. Everyone in the city is urged to take extraordinary precautions. He has been seen, or reported seen, in several places, and the police are active in investigating all leads. They hope to have him in custody within a matter of hours. He is described as —"

"Nuts," said Tracy, glad that he was off duty and not chasing a homi with the rest of the boys.

Carl Lambert, Carl Lambert . . . Oh, yes. He had been arrested three, four years ago after those Blake Street killings, the nice ones with the knife.

Hmmm, Tracy thought, maybe he ought to phone in and ask if there was anything he could do to help in the hunt. He stood up again, but the very movement made him decide he'd better not phone Headquarters. Heck, he was off duty, anyway, and they could get along without him — he hoped.

Chapter II: Tracy Wakes Up

The outer door opened. Tracy turned to see who had entered the saloon. He frowned. It couldn't have been anyone he wanted to see less. For it was Jerry Crayle, reporter for the newspaper that habitually lambasted the Force and yowled for reform, their idea of reform being their own party in power.

Crayle grinned. "Well, if it isn't Mortimer Tracy, and high as a kite. How's the rest of the Force?"

Tracy glowered at the newspaperman. It was a good thing that a few drinks didn't make Tracy pugnacious, or he would have taken a poke at Crayle's smug puss just for having the crust to call him Mortimer. Yes, that was the name his parents had misguidedly given him, but that was a long time ago and he had lived it down, except for the records.

"Lissen, you—" he said.

"Hi, Joe," said Crayle, turning his head, "What have you been feeding the police force?" Then as his eyes lit on the bottle on the bar, "Golden Eagle? Make mine the same, and fill up Tracy's."

The bald bartender went behind the bar again, and set another glass on it.

"Sure, Mr. Crayle. Water wash?"

"Not any for me, Joe," said Tracy, "I wouldn't drink with that punk if—"

Joe grinned and filled Tracy's glass anyway.

"Make the drinks on me, then, so you two can bury the hatchet," he said.

"In my head," said Tracy. "That's where he'll bury it. With an article on—"

"No, he won't, Tracy," said Joe pacifically. "You're off duty, ain't you? So you got a right."

"Sure, Tracy," affirmed Crayle. "I'm off duty, too, incidentally, and am I not tarring myself with the same brush? Ahh—and a very good brush it is. Now if all tavern owners were like Joe Hummer here and didn't refill their bottles with bootleg the minute they get down past the halfway mark—"

"There ain't any halfway mark on a whiskey bottle," said Tracy. "But, yeah, if all tavern keepers were like Joe here, then that yella newspaper of yours wouldn't have anything to squawk about. Anyway, we been tryin' to tell you, bootleg alky's not in the department of the city police. It belongs to—"

"Sure, sure. Revenue. But how about crimes it leads to? How about the guys this Coldoni ring has bumped off because they wouldn't play ball? Murder's your department, no matter why it—"

"Aw, go lay an egg," said Tracy. "There've been three unsolved killings that might've been the Coldoni mob, but nobody can prove it. Not even the *Blade,* Crayle. And when one of them was one of our own men, if you think we didn't *try —*"

"Sure, sure," said Crayle. "Now that that's off your chest, will you have one on me?"

"Well . . ." said Tracy.

"Special bulletin," said the radio as a jazz band came to the end of a down-beat. "Carl Lambert, the escaped homicidal maniac, is reported to have been seen near Sixth and Wabash half an hour ago. He wore, at that time, a gray suit and a hat, both of which were too small for him. Apparently he has been able to exchange the uniform in which he escaped for civilian garb. Police are closing in on the district surrounding Sixth and Wabash. People living near there are advised to keep doors and windows locked, and not to answer any—"

"Say," said Joe. "That's near here."

Something seemed to explode inside Tracy's head.

"Good tripe!" he said. "That guy I brought in!"

He and Joe looked at each other.

"What guy?" Crayle wanted to know.

"Got your gun, Tracy?" Joe asked.

Tracy shook his head, already sliding off the stool and wishing he'd had just one drink less.

Joe yanked a drawer open somewhere behind the bar and came out with a short-barreled heavy revolver in his hand, and a scowl on his face. He and Tracy made for the door to the back room almost abreast. The door was ajar, but from the barroom all that could be seen was a table.

"Hey!" called the reporter. "What goes on? Let me in on—"

That was when they heard the scream.

It came from somewhere quite a distance away, but it was a piercing feminine shriek that cut the air like a knife. It hung for an instant on high E, then choked off abruptly.

The kitchen was empty. The door at the back of it leading to the quarters behind the tavern stood open.

"Good gosh!" said Joe. "I thought that was locked!"

Tracy, now in the lead, plowed on through into the rooms beyond. There were two of them, and they were empty. The door at the back of the second room, leading to a small cement-paved yard, stood wide open.

Joe caught up the Headquarters detective and grabbed his arm as they reached the yard.

"Take it easy, guy," he said. "You ain't got a gun, and this ain't no picnic. If that *was* the nut—well, there were knives in that room."

"Sure," said Tracy.

A knife, of course. That was what the guy was after. That was why he had wanted to eat instead of drink. He wouldn't be hungry yet if he had escaped only late in the afternoon—not hungry enough anyway to risk bumming a meal.

"Lord, what a sap I was!" Tracy groaned.

There was a light half a block down the alley, a pale yellow spot in the gray dusk. Two houses down the alley toward the light lay the sprawled bodies of two men. Each lay in the center of a dark sticky pool that seemed to be still spreading.

Tracy got almost to them, then grabbed the top of a fence to hold on. He felt sick, physically and mentally. He heard Crayle's voice behind him.

"Where's the woman who screamed? There'll be another body, in a yard or house or—"

"Shut up," said Tracy. He didn't want to think about that possibility. "Joe, go phone the station. I'll look . . . Hey, gimme!"

He grabbed the revolver out of the tavern keeper's hand and started running up the alley toward the light, around and past the corpses of the men. Up there at the other end of the alley, past the yellow light, he had caught sight of a moving figure.

The sheer forward momentum of Tracy's pistoning legs kept him erect—for a while. Then the curb on the left came too close and got under Tracy's feet and tripped him. The corner of a garage came straight for his face. It was like a slow-motion dream of flying. He tried to throw up a hand to ward it off, but the cornerpost of the garage came faster than his hand could move. It got larger and larger until it filled his whole field of vision, and his hand had hardly moved yet. Then a red flash, into blackness. . . .

The nurse looked down and saw that Tracy's eyes were open between the bandage across his forehead and the thicker bandage across his nose.

"A Captain Burton to see you, Mr. Tracy," she said. "Do you feel well enough to see him?"

"Arrgh," said Tracy, looking at her somberly.

It was hardly a courteous affirmative, nor even a courteous negative for that matter. The nurse was a good-looking one, too, with bright red hair and a smile. From the smile, Tracy decided she didn't know anything about him or who he was.

He'd had his eyes open for half an hour now and they were just beginning to focus properly. His head felt as if it had been used as a concrete mixer and his mouth felt like the inside of a sewer after a long dry spell.

He didn't want to see anybody. He didn't even want his own company. In fact, he particularly did not want himself around, but there didn't seem to be anything he could do about that.

"I beg your pardon?" said the nurse brightly.

"Uh," said Tracy. "Aw, send him in." Might as well get it over with. He tried to turn his head, and wished he hadn't. "Hey, wait a minute. First tell me what's all wrong with me."

But the nurse had already left.

While he waited, Tracy experimentally flexed his arms a bit, then his legs. Nothing seemed to hurt as long as he didn't move his head. He ran cautiously exploring hands along his ribs, and they seemed to be intact. Then, gently, he raised his hands to his face.

Most of it was covered with bandages. His chin stuck out the bottom and seemed to work all right on its hinges, but there wasn't any doubt about his nose being broken. There was plaster under the bandage across it. As far as he could tell with his tongue, all his teeth seemed to be there.

Footsteps beside the bed made him look up. Big, red-faced Captain Burton stood there looking down at him. His eyes didn't look any too friendly. "The conquering hero," he said.

"Hi, Cap," said Tracy. "Yeah, I—I guess I did pull a boner all right. But I hadn't seen a paper or anything, so I didn't know there was a homi on the . . . Say, get him yet?"

"Not a smell of him."

Tracy groaned. "How many, so far?"

"Just the two. He must be holed up somewhere till it cools down."

"Just two, Cap? How about the woman who screamed. Didn't she—"

"Nope. Turned out she didn't see Lambert. She screamed when she came across the bodies, taking a short cut home from the store through the alley. She ran on in a building and up to her flat."

"Uh," said Tracy. "Who were the guys?"

"One wasn't much loss," said Burton. "Buck Miller, used to be a Coldoni mobster. You remember him, I guess. Other chap— his name was Randall—was a grocer, had his store there."

"Buck Miller," said Tracy wonderingly. "What was he doing there?"

The captain looked irritated.

"What's it matter? It's a public alley. There are a couple of taverns there with back entrances on it."

"Did you check 'em yet?"

"No. Why should we? What do we care what he was doing in the alley?"

"I dunno," Tracy admitted. "Guess I'm still going in circles. What's wrong with me, besides a broken smeller?"

"Bruises and contusions," said Burton. "And a suspension."

"Hey! I wasn't on duty, Cap. On my own time I got a right to . . . Well, anyway, I don't drink anything often, do I? And I could name a few of the boys who do a lot oftener than —"

"So could I," cut in Captain Burton dryly, "but they don't buy drinks for homicidal maniacs on the loose."

"But how'd I know . . . Aw, skip it. How long's the suspension?"

"There'll be a hearing before the board, tomorrow morning at ten. You ought to be out of here by then. If not, we give you a postponement."

Tracy sighed. "Okay, okay. But say, a hearing's usually pretty serious stuff, isn't it?"

"It usually is," said Burton. "I have a hunch this one won't be an exception, Tracy. Well, I got to go now. Don't worry about it — until you read the papers."

Tracy lay there staring at the ceiling, after Burton had left. Finally, he reached over and got a cord with a buzzer-button on the end of it. He pushed the button and nothing happened. After half a minute he pushed it again. And when nothing continued to happen, he held the button down steadily until the nurse appeared in the doorway.

"Yes, Mr. Tracy?" she asked.

"Will you get me a paper? This morning's *Blade?*"

"Just a minute. There'll be one in the waiting room, unless someone's thrown it away already. But the evening papers will be out soon. Wouldn't you just as soon wait until —"

"Huh-uh. It's the *Blade* I want to see in particular."

Chapter III: Trouble at Twilight

While the nurse was gone, Tracy experimented with his neck, and found he could turn his head. Encouraged, he raised himself to a sitting position and propped the pillow on end against the head of the bed, to be in a better position for reading.

He decided that he probably would live, after all. The pain from his nose was only a dull throb that could be ignored, and the headache was merely a matter of time.

A copy of the *Blade,* rather the worse for wear and with the sections out of order, was put in his lap by the nurse.

"Anything else I can bring you?" she asked brightly.

"Naw," said Tracy. "I mean, no, thanks. Unless maybe I better have an anesthetic while I read about . . . Skip it. I was kidding."

The sports section was on top, with a headline about a four-teen inning tie between the Reds and the Giants. He put it regretfully aside, and hunted out the front page.

The main banner head was by Mars out of Europe, but the Lambert case story was not hard to find. It was topped by a four-column head:

HOMICIDAL MANIAC STILL AT LARGE
SLAYS TWO IN DOWNTOWN ALLEY

And the three-column sub-head in 24-point Goudy Bold:

Headquarters Detective Gives Killer
Access to Lethal Weapon

Tracy winced a little. He closed his eyes and opened them and the sub-head was still there. Maybe he *should* have asked the redhead for an anesthetic to go with the newspaper. Well, the story itself couldn't be any worse than the heading, so he read on:

Carl Lambert, 37, homicidal maniac who escaped at four o'clock yesterday afternoon from Belleview Asylum, killed two men last night at about 7:40 p.m. and is still at large. The victims were Walter (Buck) Miller, 35, of 115 Beecher Street, and H.J. Randall, 44, grocer, of 330 Corey Street.

Both killings took place in the alley between Corey and Main Streets, at a point approximately behind the grocery store and living quarters of Randall. A knife, presumably one stolen from the back room of the tavern of Joe Hummer, 324 Corey Street, was the weapon used by the homicidal killer.

"Huh," said Tracy. " 'Homicidal killer.' That guy Crayle needs lessons in English."

The bodies were first seen by Mrs. E. Scarlotti, who lives on the second floor at 334 Corey Street. She screamed and ran upstairs to phone the police. Her screams aroused the attention of—

Tracy's eyes skipped down a few lines and caught the sub-head in minion bold:

Police Detective Aids Maniac

He gritted his teeth and read on from there:

The maniac was unwittingly aided by Mortimer Tracy, 41, Headquarters detective. Tracy, who was in an exhilarated condition, had been accosted in Corey Street, shortly prior to the murders, by Carl Lambert, who posed as a panhandler asking for money. Instead of taking Lambert in charge for begging, which was the detective's duty as a public officer, even though he was not on duty at the time, Tracy took him into the tavern of Joe Hummer, and instructed Hummer . . .

There was more of it, much more. That was just the start, and it got worse. Much worse. Tracy had read it through twice and was staring at a hole in the wall by the foot of his bed when the nurse came back.

"How do you feel, Mr. Tracy?" she asked.

Tracy looked at her suspiciously. "Swell," he said. "Why?"

"I was wondering if you'd read the editorial page, too."

"Huh?" said Tracy, and glowered at her. "What's it to you, anyway?"

"Nothing, but—"

"But what?"

"It's none of my business, of course. But if you just read that article, you're feeling very sorry for yourself, aren't you?"

"Well—"

"Sure you are. I don't blame you, in a way. It was sheer bad luck. You might take a few drinks a thousand times and nothing like that would—"

"I haven't taken a few drinks a thousand times," said Tracy. "That was the first time in—well, in years. And, of all the people in town, he had to go and pick *me*."

"That's what I mean," said the red-headed nurse. "You're still sorry for yourself. If you read that editorial, you might get mad and do something about it."

"Do what?"

"Maybe find Carl Lambert—before he kills anyone else."

"How?"

"The newspaper said you were a detective."

"But listen," said Tracy. "The whole department's after him. An organized search. What could *I* do?"

"I don't know. I merely suggested that you might read that editorial about yourself. Maybe you'd find it funny, or maybe—"

"Okay, okay, okay," said Tracy.

He began to look through the disordered newspaper. He heard the door close, just as he found the editorial in question.

He read the first half of it only. . . .

It was twilight again when Tracy left the hospital and as he walked down the street there was a tendency, at first, for him to wobble and to weave from one side of the walk to the other. But by the time he had gone a dozen blocks and was nearing the vicinity of Corey and Third Streets, Tracy got that straightened out.

He was pretty well straightened out about what he was going to do, too, although there were a lot of "ifs" to that. What the second step would be depended on where the first took him, and the third depended on the second. Yeah, naturally. He was going to do the unnatural thing for a case like this by conducting a natural investigation.

That was the one thing which, according to what Cap Burton had said, the police had not done. Undoubtedly, they had drawn a beautiful dragnet, and undoubtedly they had every available radio car at a strategic spot ready to investigate reports of a tall, thin man in ill-fitting clothes seen at such and such a place. And probably, with every housewife in the city scared stiff, there were plenty of such reports for them to investigate.

But there was one thing they had not done, apparently. They had assumed — undoubtedly correctly — that the crimes were the motiveless slayings of a homi on the loose. And that once he had committed them, he had lammed out, and only a fortune-teller could guess where he would strike again. Sure, that was right.

But — and it was the only "but" which gave Tracy a chance to work off what that editorial had done to him — they had probably ignored the very things that are strictly routine on any other murder case. They had not checked up on the scene of the crime, and the witnesses, and probably they had not bothered to check what the victims were doing at that time and place.

Of course, if this Randall guy lived there and ran a grocery there, that would not be hard to explain. But "Buck" Miller didn't live there. What had he been doing there?

And what, another part of Tracy's mind wanted to know, did it matter what he was doing there? How could it help to find where this Carl Lambert was *now?*

"Shut up," said Tracy, to that questioning voice in his mind.

If he took that attitude, he had no way to start in on things. He might as well wander about the streets at random, hoping for lightning to strike him. What if he couldn't see what things like that had to do with finding Lambert? Heck, nine-tenths of the time there didn't seem to be any reason for going through the routine steps in solving a crime, until suddenly you asked an ordinary question and got an answer you didn't expect.

It was almost twenty-four hours after — well, after what happened twenty-three hours ago. Fifteen hours before ten o'clock tomorrow morning. But fifteen hours from now would be time enough to think about that.

Let's see. It had been right about here that the guy had come up to him and bummed him for money. Had he seen the guy before that?

Tracy stood there, thinking, forcing his mind back through what seemed to be heavy fog. Sure, he remembered now. The thin man stepped out of that very doorway.

Tracy walked up to the door. It was locked, and there was a "Store for Rent" sign behind the glass panel. Well, it was a million-to-one shot, but he couldn't overlook even that odds-on a bet.

He took a ring of skeleton keys out of his pocket and found one that opened the door. He looked in, using his flashlight, and saw he need not have been suspicious. Dust was thick on the floor, and it had not been disturbed in weeks. Lambert had not been in there — before or after. He had merely waited in the doorway for a sucker to come along.

Tracy strolled on slowly, thinking.

A Mrs. Scarlotti, second floor at 334 Corey, a few doors down from Joe's, had, according to the newspaper account, discovered the bodies, and had screamed before she ran in to phone for the police. That scream had been what had sent him and Hummer and Crayle out into the alley.

Tracy turned in at Number 334 and climbed a flight of steps to the second floor. He rapped on the door at the head of the stairs.

Footsteps approached the inside of the door.

"Who's there?" a woman's voice called.

"Headquarters detective," said Tracy. "Are you Mrs. Scarlotti? Just want to ask you a few questions, about last night."

"I . . . My husband isn't here, I—I can't open the door. The papers and the radio tell us not to open unless we know—"

"Sure," said Tracy. "Wait a minute."

He took his identification card out of his wallet and slid it under the door. It was pulled on inward, and in a moment the door opened. Tracy took back the card and leaned against the door post as he replaced it in his wallet.

"Will you tell me just how you happened to discover the bodies, Mrs. Scarlotti?"

"Why, sure, but—" She looked at him, not so much suspicious this time as curious. "But four times I told the whole story. To your Mr. Burton, and to—"

Tracy nodded. "Yes, of course. But Captain Burton was taken off the case, and I wanted to hear your story myself. Of course, he told me most of it before they took him away but—"

"Took him away? Why, what—"

"Oh, nothing serious, Mrs. Scarlotti. Appendicitis. But they operated right away and got it in time. So, if you don't mind running over the story once more—"

Obviously, Mrs. Scarlotti didn't mind at all. And obviously

she had told the story a great deal more often than four times. That number, of course, had not counted friends and neighbors. And, like a snowball rolling downhill, the story had gained length with each telling.

Her reasons for having returned from the store, and which store it was and all she had purchased, seemed to go back almost to the time she had married Scarlotti. And Scarlotti was a window-cleaner by trade and she always worried for fear he would fall. Even that fact was woven into the story. But Tracy listened patiently, and learned nothing of importance.

He leaned for a while against the other side of the doorway, and then back where he had been, and wished he had gone in and sat down to listen.

Finally the torrent of words slowed down.

"Uh, thanks," he said. "I guess that's about all I need to know. You — uh — told it so well, you didn't leave any questions for me to ask."

He took a step backward and started to turn. Then he said:

"Oh, by the way. You said you told your story four times. Who did you tell besides Captain Burton?"

"Oh, the other three were reporters. They were the ones that were really interested. Mr. Burton just wanted to know whether I'd seen which way the killer ran, and I hadn't seen him at all. I had a hard time making Mr. Burton listen. But the other three men were nice. One was a Mr. Crayle from the *Blade,* and the other two from the *Sentinel.*"

"Two from the *Sentinel?* Did they come together? No, of course not, or you wouldn't have said four times you told the story. But why did the *Sentinel* send two men?"

She looked at him, her eyes a bit puzzled.

"You know, I never thought to ask. Well, maybe the explanation is something like your case. I mean, the police sending two men."

"Hmmm," said Tracy. "It might be interesting if it was. Do you recall their names?"

"The first was — I believe his name was Smithson or something like that. Not very tall, and wore thick glasses."

"Smithens," said Tracy. "I know him. The other?"

"He called late this afternoon. His name — I believe it was Riley. Yes, I'm sure it was. Walter Riley."

"I can't quite place him," said Tracy honestly. "I thought I knew all the *Sentinel's* leg-men. What'd he look like?"

"Well, I'd say he was about thirty. About your height — no, a little less. But he was stockily built, weighed almost as much as you do. Kind of yellowish complexion. I didn't notice the color of his eyes. But he had dark hair, and kind of bushy eyebrows. He wore a dark brown suit, and I think a yellow shirt. That's what made me notice his complexion. I guess that's all I can remember."

"You've got a swell memory," said Tracy. "Did he show you any credentials? I suppose he did, though, or you wouldn't have let him in."

"I — I don't believe he did," Mrs. Scarlotti said thoughtfully. "I was sweeping the stairs when he came, so there just wasn't any question of opening the door for him, and I don't believe I asked for credentials. I could see right away that he didn't look anything like those descriptions of this Carl Lambert. And, anyway, he looked familiar. I think I've seen him around."

"Around here? Nearby?"

"I think so. Say, you don't mean you think that he — that he wasn't what he said he was, or that he was dangerous?"

"Not at all, ma'am, not at all," said Tracy. "I just thought I knew all the reporters in town and I was trying to place him. But just the same, you stick to that idea of yours of not opening the door unless you know who's there. It's a good idea. Well, thanks lots."

Chapter IV: Long-shot Gamble

Mortimer Tracy walked down the stairs more slowly and thoughtfully than he had gone up them, and when he went into Joe Hummer's tavern he merely waved at Joe and crossed to the telephone on the wall. He dialed the number of the *Sentinel,* and asked to talk to Walter Riley.

"Sorry," said the operator. "We have no Mr. Riley here."

"He works days," said Tracy. "I didn't think I'd catch him there now, but maybe you can tell me how I can reach him."

"We have no Walter Riley here, sir. Day or night. There's a Mr. William Riley in Circulation. He's not here now, but—"

"I could have got the first name wrong," said Tracy. "Is this William Riley a stockily-built dark-haired man of about thirty?"

"No, sir. He's quite an elderly gentleman. I have a list of all employees here, and there is no—"

"Guess I just made a mistake, Sister. Never mind, and thanks."

He put the receiver back on the hook and walked over to the bar.

"Tracy," said Joe, "you look like something the cat dragged in. Have a drink?"

"Sure. Lemon soda, unless you got some coffee hot, maybe."

"Got coffee. With or without?"

"Black. Say, this is about the time I was in here last night. Maybe the same news program's on. Turn on the radio, Joe. I want to see if there's anything new on Lambert."

Joe nodded and flipped the switch before he went back after the coffee. The European news was still on when he came back with it.

"Listen, Tracy," Joe said, "I read that *Blade* business, and I wouldn't blame you if you're sore at Crayle. But he'll probably be in here in a few minutes and—well, don't start any trouble, will you?"

"He'll be in here? How come?"

"I mean he probably will. He eats downtown after work—his shift ends at six-thirty—and generally drops in here for a few minutes on his way home, see? About this time, like last night. But listen, if you pop him one it'll just make things worse."

"Okay," said Tracy. "There's the door now. Is it—"

Joe glanced up. "Yeah," he said. "Hullo, Mr. Crayle."

"Hi, Joe—Tracy." The reporter came on up to the bar, not too confidently. "Say, Tracy, I hope you don't think there was anything personal in that article. I didn't—"

"Sure," said Tracy. "Shut up."

"I want you to know I didn't write that editorial."

"Shut up, I said," Tracy snapped. "I want to catch this broadcast."

He missed the first words. The voice on the radio was just saying: "—are still searching for Carl Lambert, the escaped maniac who killed two men last night. The activities of the Police Department are under severe criticism by—"

"Shut it off, Joe," said Tracy. "Just wanted to be sure nothing new had come in. Listen—you, too, Crayle. I wasn't exactly myself last night. Were there any angles you know of that got overlooked, maybe?"

Crayle looked at him curiously. "What do you mean, angles?"

"You sound like you got something, Tracy," Joe said. "Give."

Tracy shook his head slowly.

"Huh-uh. Well, maybe I got something, but I don't know what it is. Listen, do you know anyone fits this? About five feet nine or ten; heavily built; sallow skin, dark hair and bushy eyebrows. Yesterday he wore a dark brown suit and yellow shirt. Might be a newspaperman or might not."

Joe's eyes widened.

"What could another guy have to do with this Lambert? Another nut or something? That's silly."

"Yeah," Tracy admitted. "But do you know a guy like I described? Or you, Crayle?"

"Um," said Crayle. "No newspaperman, Tracy. Unless Ronson of the *Sentinel*. No, you wouldn't call his eyebrows bushy, and anyway I saw him yesterday and he wore blue serge. But, say, how about Hank Widmer?"

Tracy whistled. Then he drained the last of his coffee and stood up.

"Hey," said Joe, "let us in on it. What could Hank Widmer have to do—with Carl Lambert?"

"I haven't an idea," Tracy told him. "But I hanker to know."

"You mean a guy described like that was seen around here or something yesterday? But how would that tie him in with a homi killing a couple people?"

Tracy grinned. "I was kidding you, Joe. It wasn't yesterday. It was today, this afternoon."

"But there haven't been any murders today."

"Not yet," said Tracy.

He went out, leaving them staring at him.

It had been a nice exit, Tracy realized as he reached the sidewalk, but it would have been less spectacular if Joe and Crayle had known that he didn't really know a thing. He wasn't even guessing yet. He was merely trying to guess.

And there didn't seem to be even an intelligent guess that would tie up Carl Lambert and Hank Widmer, except through Buck Miller, one of the men Lambert had killed. Hank Widmer —and that was the reason Tracy had whistled—was Buck Miller's pal. Both members, or they had been not so long ago, of the Coldoni mob.

All right, where did that get him? A homicidal maniac, who was not and never had been a criminal in the ordinary sense of the word, who could not possibly be tied up with gangsters, had escaped from an asylum. Thus far he had killed two men, one of whom was a Coldoni gangster. The other was a grocer. And where would a grocer fit in?

Tracy swore and began to walk slower so that — he hoped — he could think better. What did it matter that the other guy was a grocer, or that Miller was a crook? A homicidal maniac didn't ask questions or care whom he killed, did he?

But then why had Hank Widmer gone to see Mrs. Scarlotti this afternoon, posing as a reporter in order to question her?

Maybe it hadn't been Hank Widmer. That description was general enough to fit quite a few guys, of course. But if it wasn't Widmer, then Tracy didn't have a lead. Yes, for the sake of seeing where it got him, he would assume that Widmer had called on Mrs. Scarlotti.

Where did that get him? Nowhere.

Except that his feet were taking him in the direction of the garage where he kept his car, and the only reason he could have for wanting that car would be to drive out to the Green Dragon, where one would be most likely to run into Coldoni. Or Hank Widmer. And most likely to run into trouble. If he tried arresting or questioning people without knowing even what questions he wanted to ask them.

Then he laughed. Trouble? He couldn't be in any worse trouble, short of occupancy of a slab at the morgue, than he was in right now, could he?

He began to walk faster. But by the time he had driven the car out of the garage, he realized that it was still a bit early for the Green Dragon. He drove slowly and roundabout, thinking. The thinking, too, was slow and roundabout. If Hank Widmer had impersonated a reporter to question the woman who had discovered the bodies of Miller and Randall, then it meant there was something fishy.

But what? It was absurd to think of a tie-up between Carl Lambert and the alky ring. Could it be that. . . . But no, there was no doubt about the identity of the tall man he, Tracy, had taken into Joe Hummer's to buy a drink. There had been a picture of Carl Lambert in the *Blade,* and there wasn't any doubt about identity.

The doorman at the Green Dragon did not recognize Tracy at first. Then he grinned as though the plaster cast on the detective's nose was funnier than Charlie Chaplin.

"If you like it that much," Tracy said, "maybe I could arrange for you to have one too. Is your best customer here?"

The doorman pretended not to understand.

"Who?" he wanted to know.

Tracy glowered at him, and walked on in. He stopped at the cigar counter and took his time about buying cigarettes and lighting one of them. He knew Coldoni was there. His car had been outside across the street. And there was a communicator that the doorman could use in talking to the barman in the main room at the rear.

The doorman had understood him all right, and he would phone back that a man from Headquarters was looking for Coldoni. And if Coldoni made himself scarce, it might mean that he didn't want to be found, that he had something on what would be his conscience if he had one.

That would tell Tracy something, even if he didn't know what. And if Coldoni scrammed—well, there wasn't anything Tracy was ready to ask him anyway. Maybe there would be after he had seen Widmer.

But Coldoni, dapper and supercilious as ever, was lounging against the bar. He turned, as Tracy walked in, and smiled with his lips.

"Ah," he said, "the conquering hero, with the scars of battle."

Tracy walked on past him without a word or a glance and opened the door to the room behind the bar. Nothing he could have said to Coldoni, he knew, would get his goat as much as

ignoring him It was imagination, of course, but he
thought he could feel the cold, angry stare of Coldoni on the back
of his neck.

There were four men sitting around a card table in the back
room, one of them Hank Widmer. The game had just started,
apparently, and was being played desultorily for small stakes until
more players, suckers preferred, should join the game.

Tracy ignored the others.

"Hullo, Widmer," he said. "Want to talk to you."

Widmer was wearing, Tracy noticed, a dark brown suit and
a shirt that was almost yellow.

Widmer glanced up at Tracy insolently, then turned back to
the game, lifting up the corner of the hole card he had just been
dealt and leaning backward to peer at its under side.

"Go ahead," he said. "I can listen while I play."

"Not here," said Tracy. "Down at the station. Some of the other
boys have questions to ask you, too."

"You wouldn't mean this is an arrest?"

"That's just what I would mean."

The dealer, with an ace up, tossed in a red chip.

"Too much," Widmer said, and turned down his up card. Then
he looked at Tracy again. "What for?"

"Suspicion," Tracy told him. "Suspicion of anything you want
to be suspected of. Want to come along willingly? I'd just as soon
you didn't myself."

He heard footsteps and knew that Coldoni had left the bar
and come over to the doorway.

"Looking for trouble, copper?" Coldoni's soft voice said.

"I'd love it," said Tracy, without turning.

Coldoni chuckled. "Go with the guy, Hank," he said. "He hasn't
got anything on us. And I'll have a mouthpiece there by the time
you get there. He can't hold you."

"Thanks, boys," Tracy said. "That's too, too swell of you."

He stepped backward and his heel came down on the pointed toe of Coldoni's shoe.

"Oops, sorry," Tracy said, but he threw his weight the wrong way for an instant before he recovered his balance and stepped sideward.

Coldoni's face was white as Tracy jerked around to face him, and his hand had gone, almost as though unconsciously, toward his lapel. But Tracy's own hand was already inside his coat, and Coldoni's froze where it was, then dropped. But his thin, white face looked like a devil mask.

"Curse you, copper," he said.

Tracy grinned. "I am an awkward lummox, ain't I? Even the newspapers think so. Ready, Widmer, or shall I—"

The sallow-complexioned man stood up and put his chips into his coat pocket.

"I'll keep these, boys," he said. "Back in an hour or two. Hold my seat." He strolled toward Tracy.

"If you got a heater, better park it," Tracy said. "The boys at Headquarters might not like your carrying one. They're funny that way."

Deliberately he turned his back on both Widmer and Coldoni and started for the door. But he took only two steps, then stopped and waited. Those two steps brought him to a point where he could see behind him in the glass of a picture that hung on the wall beside the door. It was not a mirror, but the picture was a glossy print and the light shone on it diagonally. In the glass, he could see both men.

No gun exchanged hands as Widmer passed his chief. Apparently Widmer was not packing one. But his hand darted to the breast pocket of his coat and flipped out a small leather-bound notebook. Coldoni took it and slid it into his own pocket.

Tracy let it go. That notebook would be some addresses of customers of the alky ring, but the police knew most of them already. It would not be proof of anything, and anyway Tracy was not interested in alky tonight. Not unless he could find out how—if at all—alky without tax concerned Carl Lambert.

At the door he turned and said:

"Don't count on getting him back too soon, Coldoni. It's tough to get habeas corpus on a murder rap."

He watched Coldoni's face, and Widmer's for reaction. But there was not a sign of anything except bewilderment, and possibly a bit of relief. And both looked genuine, but you couldn't tell.

Widmer grinned. "I'll phone and let you know who I'm supposed to've murdered, Chief," he said. "So long."

Before Tracy got into the car, he frisked Widmer to be sure about a gun. Widmer was not heeled.

Tracy headed the car toward Third and Corey Streets. If there was a light showing at the Scarlotti place, he would take Widmer up there and get Mrs. Scarlotti to identify him as her caller of the afternoon. Then it would be tougher for Widmer to wriggle out of explaining.

He swung the car in at the curb in front of Joe Hummer's. If the Scarlotti place was dark, Tracy had another idea that involved the use of Joe's telephone. He was still working in the dark, and maybe hunting in the dark for a black cat that was not there, but he had a hunch something might happen if he kept throwing monkey wrenches into the machinery.

One monkey wrench would be the fact that Widmer, whether or not he talked, would not show up any more tonight, either back at the Green Dragon or at Headquarters where a mouthpiece would be waiting to spring him.

"You're waiting for me a minute here, Hank," Tracy said. "And just to keep you from getting ideas—"

He took out his handcuffs and snapped one of them around Widmer's left wrist, the other to the steering post.

"What the devil are we doing here?" Widmer demanded. "Don't tell me you're going to leave me here and go in there to get tanked up."

Tracy grinned at him, but didn't answer. He got out of the car and walked up to 334 Corey, and into the areaway alongside the building. There wasn't any light on the second floor. He mumbled something, and went up and rang the bell anyway.

After a couple of minutes a small, wiry Italian with curly black hair came to the door, dressed in an old bathrobe. He was about half the size of the woman Tracy had talked to.

"Mr. Scarlotti?" Tracy asked, and showed his badge. "Police. Awful sorry if you have to wake your wife, but I'd like her to identify someone I have in the car. I'll bring him up, when she's ready."

The wiry little man shook his head. "Elda, she's-a not here. She's-a very upset about finding those men stabbed. I send her spend a few days with her sister in Buffalo. She no feel-a good."

Hummph, thought Tracy, she had pulled a fast one to wangle herself a vacation. She had *enjoyed* the excitement and having something to talk about. She feel-a swell. But if she was gone, that was that.

"Well," he said, "sorry if I waked you up."

"But who you wan-a her to see? She no see guy who stabbed —"

"Naw, I know that," Tracy said. "Another guy — one who came here to talk to her today. Said he was a reporter and gave her a phony name."

"So? For what?"

"I dunno, yet," admitted Tracy. "Maybe you could guess?"

The wiry little man shook his head slowly.

"But," he said helpfully, "if he talk-a to my Elda and tell-a her he's . . . Say, I go down and punch-a his face and make-a him tell why he —"

Tracy grinned. "Thanks, but I've thought of that myself. I can handle it." He turned away, then remembered the monkey wrench policy. "The guy," he said, "is a member of Coldoni's mob. That suggest anything?"

Again Scarlotti shook his head slowly.

"No. But then maybe it's-a not so good idea to punch his face."

Tracy laughed. "It's still a good idea. Well, so long, and thanks."

He shouldn't, he realized, have mentioned the Coldoni angle. Now, if it came to a point of Mrs. Scarlotti having to identify Widmer, he would have to get in touch with her somehow before her husband saw her. Obviously the Italian had a normal fear of getting in wrong with gangsters and would advise his wife not to stick her neck out.

But Scarlotti's reaction had been natural. He had not pretended not to know who the gangster was, nor given any other cause to be suspected.

Chapter V: Dead End

Business was picking up in Joe Hummer's tavern. Crayle was still at the bar, occupying the same stool he had been sitting on when Tracy had left a couple of hours ago.

"Hi, Tracy," Crayle said. "How's about another cup of coffee? Or are you on the wagon again?"

Joe came back from waiting on one of the tables.

"Hullo, Tracy," he said. "Have something on Crayle? He's got the zipper open on his weasel-sack."

Tracy shook his head. "Just want to use your phone, Joe. Got a friend waiting for me outside."

"Bring him in." suggested Crayle.

He and Joe turned their heads to look out through the glass at Tracy's car. "What the heck, Tracy?" Crayle said. "That's—"

"Name no names," Tracy interrupted. "He's bashful. He'd rather stay out there."

He took his notebook out of his vest pocket and flipped through it to find the number he intended to call, then walked back to the telephone before Crayle could ask any more questions.

It was a local toll call, to the sheriff of an outlying village twenty miles from town, a man who was a good friend of Tracy's. The detective pitched his voice low so Crayle would not hear the number or the message.

"Hey, Tracy," called Crayle, as the detective replaced the receiver and started for the door. "Let us in on it. What's up?"

"Read about it in the *Sentinel*," Tracy told him, and went on out and got back in the car.

He had driven quite some distance when suddenly Widmer looked around with narrowed, suspicious eyes.

"What the devil?" he demanded. "This isn't the way to the station."

"That's right," Tracy said gravely. "Guess I must be a bit lost. Well, we'll keep on and maybe we'll get to it."

He swung the car into an arterial that led out of the city.

"Listen, copper, there's a name for this. Kidnaping. And anyway, what's it all about?"

"Save your breath for answering questions, when I ask them."

"You'll lose your job for this, Tracy. I'll —"

"Don't make me laugh. Unless I pull a rabbit out of a hat, I haven't got any job to lose. This is my last night, and I aim to have fun."

"While you can still hide behind a badge, huh? Well, listen, if you retire tomorrow, you better pick a nice quiet island about four thousand miles from —"

"Shut up," said Tracy.

He drove on in silence, out past the last diminishing buildings of the city's outskirts. Ten miles out he swung the car into a side road, from it to a dirt road that looked as though it led to nowhere. A mile up the dirt road he stopped.

"End of the line," he said. "Get out."

"If you think you can get away with —"

Tracy put the heel of his palm in Widmer's face and pushed, hard. The gangster's head hit against the glass of the door with a thud. With his other hand, Tracy reached across and yanked down the handle of the door.

Widmer tumbled out of the car, barely managing to stay on his feet. He recovered his balance while Tracy was climbing out after him, and started a swing at the detective's face.

Tracy caught the blow on his left forearm and then jumped down off the running-board, adding the momentum of his descent to a short vicious right-hander that caught Widmer in the chest and sent him backward. He stumbled in the shallow ditch and fell.

"And now," said Tracy, "I'm not hiding behind any badge. This is strictly unofficial."

He took the badge off the under side of his coat lapel and tossed it behind him onto the seat of the car. He took his automatic out of the shoulder holster and put it with the badge.

"Try running," he said grimly, "and I'll pick up that gun again and shoot your legs from under. Otherwise it's even. Now get up."

Hank Widmer didn't. He gave vent to his feelings in some scorching remarks, but he didn't seem disposed to take advantage of Tracy's being without his badge and gun.

Tracy grinned. "Don't get up, then," he said. "The Marquis of Queensbury isn't around here anyway, so he won't know it if I kick your teeth out. If you want to talk now instead of later, that's okay too. I'll give you three chances. One. Two. Th—"

"What do you want to know, blast you?"

"That's better," said Tracy. "Where's Carl Lambert?"

"Where's. . . . Are you crazy?"

"You're supposed to answer questions, not ask them. In case you didn't understand, we'll start over on those three chances. I asked you—where's Carl Lambert? One. Two—"

"I don't know. Good glory, Tracy, I never saw the guy! I never heard of him until I read he had escaped!"

Widmer, obviously cowed, was sitting up now, drawn back as far as he could get against the fence at the roadside. He seemed to see that his only chance to avoid a beating was to talk, and once he started, he talked fast.

"Listen, Tracy, I been in town only a year, so I didn't know about the Lambert case when he was sent up. I mean, put in. What the devil makes you think I'd know anything about a homicidal—"

"There you go asking questions again," interrupted Tracy. "All right, you answer it yourself. You know I have a reason for tying you up with Lambert. You tell *me* what it could be."

"There isn't any reason, Tracy. I don't know how—"

Tracy stepped closer and said, "One. How do you like the way I look with a cast on my nose? Funny? Well, you'll look funnier with one of these *and* your front teeth out. Two. Th—"

"Wait! You mean Mrs. Scarlotti?"

"I might," Tracy admitted. "What about Mrs. Scarlotti?"

"I—oh, all right, all right. I'll start at the beginning, but it's a mare's nest. It was this guy Lambert killed them all right."

"Was it?"

"Sure. You must've found out I talked to this Scarlotti dame and jumped to the idea that there was something fishy. Well, I had something of the same idea, but—well, it wouldn't wash. I decided I'd been seeing the bogey-man."

"Just what was this idea?"

"You know well enough what I'm talking about."

"Forget what I know. You tell me."

"Well, it just seemed fishy that out of a whole city full of people, Buck Miller was the one who got bumped by a homi on the loose. It—well, it was a coincidence, that's all. But I wanted to make sure."

"How about Randall?"

"Who?"

"H.J. Randall."

"Oh, yeah, the grocer. No, there isn't any tie-up there. That's partly what made me decide the homi angle was on the up-and-up."

Tracy looked at him closely.

"That and what else?" he demanded.

"Oh, *all* of it. Your story, the way the papers gave it, and Crayle's and Hummer's and—well, it all added up. It couldn't have been anything but the loose nut, could it? You and Hummer both got a good look at him. Wasn't it this Lambert?"

Tracy ignored the question. "You thought it might not be. Who did you think might have killed Buck Miller? You knew him pretty well, didn't you?"

Widmer nodded. He was talking freely now, as though having kicked loose with what he had already said, he had nothing further to hide and was even interested in finding out if Tracy knew anything.

"Yeah, Buck Miller and me—well, I guess I was his closest friend. We worked together on—on whatever we worked on."

Tracy grinned at the circumlocution.

"You mean on carrying out whatever orders the boss gave you," he said. "We'll skip that. But did anyone have any reason for wanting Buck out of the way?"

"No." Widmer shook his head, then hesitated. "Well, I've gone this far and I might as well say that there might have been a reason I didn't know about. I had a hunch, for the last couple weeks, that Buck was holding out something on me. And he had a new dame."

"What's her name?"

"Marilyn Breese. A pony at the Troc. But she wouldn't have anything to do with it, Tracy. All I meant about her was that she was costing him plenty dough. And he had it. That isn't squealing because—what the heck, he's dead."

"You mean you think he had more money the last couple weeks than he should have had, from sources you knew about?"

"That's it. I dunno where he got it, and it don't matter now. But then when he got killed—well, it was silly I guess, but I thought maybe—"

"So you turned detective and conducted an investigation on your own hook. Coldoni know about your little idea?"

Hank Widmer shook his head again.

"Huh-uh. And listen, if it gets out about me talking to Mrs. S., I'm going to have to do some tall explaining to the boss. He'll want to know why I didn't come to him with it."

"And why didn't you?"

"Well—look, Tracy, you got some idea what things are all about. Suppose Buck had crossed the boss. Suppose it wasn't this Lambert bumped him. Who would be the next most likely guy? And would the boss like to have me doing any guessing out loud? I ask you."

Tracy thought it over a minute. It was disappointing. He'd hoped for more, something that would give him a definite lead. But what Hank Widmer had just told him made sense and it rang true. Apparently he and Hank had had the same idea. It had led Hank to a brick wall, and Tracy didn't see how he was going to get over that wall himself.

If Carl Lambert really *had* killed the gangster and the grocer, then that was that. Curse it all, he didn't have any real reason to think anything else had happened.

But that had been over twenty-four hours ago. Why hadn't the homicidal maniac struck again? According to his case history, he would not be sitting quietly in hiding, waiting for them to catch him. He was an extreme case, obsessed with an insatiable urge to slash people with a knife.

And he had a knife now. Why wasn't he using it? Or did he have a knife? Had he ever had one, that is, since his escape? Or had he escaped?

"Nuts," thought Tracy. "Pretty soon I'll be wondering if there ever was such a guy and if I really tried to buy him a drink."

Widmer's voice cut into his thoughts.

"Honest, Tracy, that's all I can tell you. The whole story. Now what the devil can I tell Coldoni about what you wanted with me, that won't spill to him that I had a wrong hunch that might not set so well with him?"

"Tell him anything," said Tracy. "Maybe by tomorrow you won't have to tell him anything. I. . . . Skip it. What was that notebook you handed Coldoni?"

Widmer's voice sounded wary. "What notebook?"

Tracy took his own notebook from his pocket, the one he had carried for a long time to jot down addresses.

"One like this," he said. "Almost exactly like it. That refresh your memory, or do I have to get tough again?"

"Oh, that," said Widmer. "Yeah. That couldn't have anything to do with this other business. Just routine. A list of addresses. You can guess what for, without my drawing a diagram."

"You mean a list of the taverns that buy alky."

"Whiskey," corrected Widmer.

"If you can call it that. If you had that list, it means you were handling either deliveries or collections—you and Buck, if he worked with you. Which?"

"Listen, Tracy, haven't I sung enough? And since when are you going in for revenue work?"

"The devil with the revenue work, for now," said Tracy. "Why'd you think I brought you out here instead of taking you in where a shorthander'd be taking down what you said? All I'm interested in right now is murder. Anything else is off the record, and anyway it would be your word against mine whether you said it or not."

"But what's this stuff got to do with murder?"

"Let me judge that. Which were you and Buck handling? Deliveries, or collections?"

"Okay, but it's off the record. Fifty-fifty. We collected for whatever we delivered. That's why I don't see how Buck could've been chiseling. Not without being caught."

"Maybe he was caught."

Widmer had stood up and was leaning against the fence now.

"Aw, Tracy, there's nothing in it," he said. "I tell you I had the same idea, but it won't wash. Assume he was chiseling, even if I can't see how. Give anybody you want to name all the reason you want to give 'em for rubbing him out. It's still true that he got bumped off by a maniac. The nut was there, wasn't he? You ought to know. He swipes a knife from Joe's kitchen and runs out the back way and stabs the first couple guys he comes across. What else can you make out of it?"

Tracy grunted. "Shut up, or you'll have me believing it."

"Don't you?"

"I don't want to," said Tracy. "Get in the car. I might be wrong, but I think you leveled with me."

"Okay. But listen, what am I going to tell the boss about why you picked on *me,* without admitting about me having the wild idea I had and seeing Mrs. Scarlotti?"

Tracy slide his automatic back into its holster and put the badge back on before he slid in under the wheel.

"You're going to have time to figure that out before you see him again," he said. "I got you fixed up for board and room till tomorrow afternoon. I want to find out what Coldoni does if he gets worried about you."

"Huh? You can't —"

"It's strictly legal. He's a sheriff, see? There's nothing illegal, if he finds you on the street in his town, about arresting you as a vag, is there? I don't think you'll have any explanation he'll believe about how you got there."

"But Tracy —"

"And of course you won't have any money or identification on you when you get out of the car." Tracy grinned. "But don't let that worry you, pal. I'll mail them back to you some time tomorrow."

Chapter VI: Death Waits in Darkness

Wearily Tracy dropped himself on the stool by the hamburger stand counter.

"Hi, Pete," he said to the tow-headed kid back of the counter. "Put a couple on, with. And coffee."

"Sure, Mr. Tracy," said the kid, and then, hesitantly: "I read about the Carl Lambert case. You sure had tough luck, Mr. Tracy. Has anything more happened since then?"

Tracy shook his head tiredly. "Had what I thought was a lead, but it petered out on me."

He glanced up at the clock. Ten minutes after one.

He stirred sugar into his coffee, took a sip, and it made him feel a little better. But not much. He was getting sleepy and his nose and his head hurt and he wished he could go home and go to sleep.

It would not be so bad, he thought disgustedly, trying to solve a case if he could feel sure there was a case to solve. But in all probability there wasn't any. Carl Lambert had committed the two motiveless murders, then lammed out across country and, for reasons of his own, had not killed anybody else yet. Or maybe he had been hit by a truck and not yet identified or something.

Or maybe —

Nuts. He had maybed himself in circles until he was dizzy. And he had undoubtedly increased the jam he was in at Headquarters by making an arrest after Cap Burton had told him he was suspended, even though the captain had not taken his gun and badge along, and then not showing up with the man he had arrested. He wondered if Coldoni's lawyer was still waiting at the station.

"Pete," he said, "murder is a funny thing. If you haven't the faintest idea what you're doing, you can always go around throwing monkey wrenches, and maybe you can get somebody worried."

The tow-headed kid put the hamburgers on the counter in front of Tracy, and looked interested.

"Yeah?" he asked. "How?"

"Murder is a guinea pig," said Tracy. "It has pups, or piglets or whatever you'd call it. A guy commits a murder and then he finds he had to kill somebody else to cover up. Maybe the second guy might be a grocer. Then if you can keep it rolling, he'd think, whether he's right or not, that he has to kill another guy to keep it quiet. Maybe a detective."

"Gee, you mean you think that —"

"No, but I wish I did."

The door opened and Tracy looked around as two men came in. "Hullo, boys," he said. "Anything new on short-wave about Lambert?"

"Huh-uh." The foremost of the two men shook his head. "But listen, Tracy, there's a broadcast out about you. We saw your car outside. The cap says you're supposed to be suspended but that you pulled an arrest at the Green Dragon, and then never showed up with the guy. A lawyer waited there a long time."

"Yeah," said Tracy. "That's why I didn't bring him in. I just wanted to talk to him. Got orders to bring me in, Harry, or what?"

Harry Lane looked uncomfortable.

"Well, suppose you call up the station from here, Tracy. See what the cap says. I don't want to. . . ."

"Okay, anything you say," said Tracy. He crossed over to the phone and talked into it for a while. His lips were a bit tight as he came back and, before he sat down again to finish his sandwiches, he took off his badge and handed it, with his gun, to the squad car men.

"It's okay," he told them. "You don't have to take me in. But the cap seemed to think I'd better not run around with these until after the hearing tomorrow morning anyway."

"Gee, Tracy, that's tough luck. I'm sorry."

"It's all right, Harry. Skip it."

While he munched the hamburgers, Tracy heard the squad car start up and drive away. He didn't say anything more to the tow-headed kid behind the counter, and the kid had wisdom enough to keep his own mouth shut.

When Tracy got back behind the wheel of his own car, he sat there and thought a while, while he unlaced the empty shoulder holster which, without a gun, made him feel strange and lopsided.

He knew he was licked, but darned if he was going to admit it, in spite of how tired he felt. He had gambled on practically kidnaping Hank Widmer, partly to see what Coldoni's reaction would be.

Well, Widmer had, in a way, disappointed him by telling what seemed to be a straight story. So it looked like he had been barking up the wrong tree, but he was going back to the Green Dragon anyway. He was going back without a gun and without authority, but Coldoni wouldn't know that.

He drove slowly, trying to think out some course of action that might force . . . Blast it, was he still hunting in the dark for a black cat that wasn't there? Well, what if he was? He hadn't anything much to lose now. And he had the rest of the night to keep on groping.

The familiar streets grew more familiar and he saw that his route across town was taking him within a block of his own place. Well, he might as well take advantage of that to leave the billfold he had taken from Hank Widmer in a safe place. There had been quite a bit of money in that wallet, and he would rather not carry it around until he had a chance to mail it.

And a bit of cold water on the accessible portions of his face ought to help wake him up and make his mind work again. A

shower? No, he had better not take time for that. It was getting
pretty late. If only his nose would stop throbbing—

He swung the car in to the curb and climbed out. He told
himself he had better hurry, but his steps up the staircase were
slow and lagging. He fumbled the key, had a lot of trouble getting
it into the keyhole in the dark, so much trouble that he lit a match
and held it in his left hand while he put in the key and turned
it with his right.

The tiny flame was dying as the door swung open toward him,
but it showed him the shadowy, unidentifiable bulk of the man
standing there just inside the door. And it caught the gleam of
the knife that slashed out toward Tracy's stomach. A kitchen knife.

It was that gleam of dim flame on dull metal that saved him.
Tracy still had hold of the door with his right hand and he
slammed it inward so the edge of it struck the arm snaking forward with the knife. The impact slowed and deflected the blow,
and as the door bounded back, Tracy grabbed into the darkness
and caught the arm of his attacker.

He threw his weight through the now open doorway, bearing
his assailant back, even as he felt the arm he held trying to twist
about for a stabbing blow into his side. He had his cheek against
his opponent's chest, and there were blows raining against his
head and neck. Painful blows, but not dangerous. In the reeling
darkness and the close quarters, the man he struggled with could
not have aim or leverage for a rabbit punch that might have ended
the fight.

As he staggered forward, not daring to step back, Tracy slid
his left hand down until it closed around the wrist of the knife-
hand. Then, risking letting go with his own right hand, he bent
lower and caught his right arm around the back of the knees of
the man he fought, and threw his own weight forward, butting
with his head.

There was a moment when they were both off-balance, then a heavy crash, and Tracy fell on top. The knife clattered against the floor. Tracy felt the man under him struggling to rise, but instead of swinging a random blow into the darkness, Tracy stuck out his hand until it felt a face. He pushed the face backward, hard and suddenly, and there was a thud against the floor. The man under him went limp.

Tracy straightened up slowly, and struck a match.

"I'll be —" he said, as it flared.

The man who had tried to kill him was Joe Hummer, the barkeeper!

It was some little time before Hummer gained consciousness, and when he did he was in no position to fight or to wield a knife. Tracy had seen to that. Nor was the barkeeper inclined to answer questions.

"Like sin I'll talk," he growled to Tracy's repeated demands. "Why should I? So you can prove I tried to kill you, and that's bad enough, but why should I stick my neck —"

"Shut up," said Tracy. "I'm telling you why. But first I'm going to finish telling you what happened. When I came into the saloon last night with an escaped homicidal maniac in tow, you recognized him, or guessed who he was, from the descriptions or maybe his picture in the newspaper. And you suddenly saw how you could get away with killing a guy you had to kill — Buck Miller."

"Nuts," said Joe. "And even if you *did* guess right —"

"I said to shut up," said Tracy. He gestured with the old service revolver he had dug up out of a trunk while Joe Hummer was still unconscious, and Joe sank back into the chair. "The reason the Feds hadn't closed on the Coldoni bunch was that they didn't know where the accounts and collections were handled. Coldoni never had any records. They had searched, unofficially.

"You were the dark horse of the gang, and probably next to Coldoni himself in power. We'll find out all about that when we

search your place, won't we, Joe? All right, but you'd been drag-
ging down on the boss and Buck Miller found it out and cut
himself in on the deal for extra cash. And he started bleeding
you worse and you wanted a way to kill him, *if* you could do it
in a way that not even Coldoni, let alone the cops, would know
he was murdered at all. Nobody figures a killing by a maniac
as a murder, the ordinary way."

Joe sighed. "Tracy, do I have to listen to all this hogwash? If
I'm under arrest, go ahead and take me in."

"You're not under arrest. I'm not even a cop any more. Listen!
Buck Miller was in the part of your building behind the kitchen,
waiting to see you. You saw your chance in Carl Lambert. When
you took him back to feed him, you stepped out a minute to see
whether he would go for a knife. You wanted to be sure who he
was.

"Then you captured him. You went on back and stalled Buck
Miller, walked with him out into the alley, and stabbed him with
the knife Lambert had tried to swipe.

"This poor grocer, Randall, is going or coming the back way,
and he'd have been a witness, so you stabbed him too. But that
was all to the good. Two killings looked more like a homicidal
maniac than one. And you were back in the tavern within ten
minutes, and you figured I was too interested in my drinks to
know you'd been gone even that long."

Tracy grinned.

"The funny part is that I never guessed," he said. "I was just
messing around tonight at random, trying to start something,
and in some way you got the idea that I was getting on to you
and that you'd better get out of the road. But you came here to
kill me, and then you'd have let Lambert go and let him get
himself caught somewhere and take the rap for all three killings,
besides any he might do on his own hook.

"But what made you think . . . Hey, I know! You knew I had Hank Widmer out in my car when I stopped back and"—Tracy laughed out loud and slapped his knees with the hand that didn't hold the revolver —"you saw that notebook of mine I got a phone number out of and you thought it was Widmer's and that I knew about your connection with the gang! Well, either pick up that pen and start writing or we're on our way."

Joe Hummer stood up. "Let's get going then."

"Okay, Joe. But not to Headquarters. I told you I'm not a cop any more. We're looking up Coldoni and I'm turning you over to *him* with the news that you killed Buck Miller and have been chiseling on him. I'll tell him to go to your place and search there and — well, he won't need a confession like the cops would, would he?"

Hummer's face turned pasty white.

"You're kidding, Tracy. He'd. . . . You wouldn't do that."

Tracy's eyes, over the bandage across the middle of his face, looked to be the color and hardness of ball-bearings.

Joe Hummer sat back slowly and gingerly in the chair, and reached for the pen and paper on the table beside him. . . .

Gray light of dawn paled the yellow aura of the lamp on Captain Burton's desk.

Tracy slumped wearily in the visitor's chair in front of that desk and talked as though each word cost him an effort.

"Yeah, so I went around and got Carl Lambert, too, so I could bring them both in while I was at it. But, you see, he didn't commit the murders at all. He was tied up in the empty building next to Joe's. And, like I told you, Hank Widmer's in the clink at Shelbyville. We can send for him there.

"I think that confession, and what else we'll find at Joe's, will give us enough to break up the whole gang. I'd have gone around and brought in Coldoni too, but —"

Captain Burton snorted. "But you thought you might want help to round up the rest of the gang?"

Tracy must have been too tired to recognize the sarcasm.

"Well, there's no hurry," he said defensively. "They don't know we want 'em, or that Joe's confession there tied up the gang with those old killings, including Molenauer's. They don't know we got Joe, and they'll be easy to pick up."

Captain Burton grinned and winked at the stenographer at the side of his desk who was taking notes of everything.

"I guess the rest of the Force can manage to take over from here, Tracy," he said. "Unless you really *want —*"

"I can, Cap, but I really ought to get a couple of hours nap before that hearing at ten."

"Hearing? What hearing? Oh, yeah. Hmmm, I don't think you need to worry about attending that, Tracy. I haven't quite the authority to squash it myself, but I can promise you the inspector will. And listen, you look really done in. I have got the authority to give you another week's leave. You better go home and sleep a couple days straight, and then"— he grinned —"then maybe you ought to go out and get plastered to celebrate."

Tracy stood up. "Thanks, Cap," he said, and stuck out his hand. "But if it's the same to you, I'll go fishing. G'night."

Captain Burton watched Tracy's broad shoulders weave down the hallway, as erratically as though liquor instead of lack of sleep and physical weariness were swaying him.

"If we had more men like that on the Force," he said to the stenographer, "we wouldn't need a Force."

The stenographer looked at him. "That doesn't quite make sense, sir."

"No," said the captain, grinning. "It doesn't, does it?"

TWO BEERS FOR TWO

It was an hour past midnight when I turned into the dark little side street and stopped near the Morris Undertaking Parlors. I recognized that sleek, shiny limousine that stood in front of the building. It was Augie Wheeler's swankiest car, bulletproof glass and all, and it meant that Little Augie was inside the mortuary. I didn't like Little Augie.

Then I remembered my job and kept on walking. Anything Little Augie does is news, and news is my job. Maybe Mac was right in thinking there'd be a story here tonight. Maybe I'd been wrong in trying to argue him into sending a sob sister instead of a police reporter.

Augie came out of the door when I was a dozen paces away. He saw me and stood there waiting. He's a big, sloppily dressed hulk of a man who looks like a broken-down prize fighter till you see his eyes; then you get an idea why. Morrelli and Jeppert came out of the door and stood beside him.

Augie said, "Hi, Slim," and his mouth smiled.

I said, "Hello, Wheeler," and tried to walk on past, but he caught my arm in a grip like a bear trap.

"What you going in there for?"

"Orders," I told him. "A story."

"I don't want a story." He let go my arm as if that took care of that, and probably he was right. The two torpedoes had moved around until they stood between me and the door of the under-taking parlors. Augie grinned. "You news hounds'll make a picnic out of the funeral tomorrow morning. Let it go till then."

I shrugged my shoulders. "I just work for the *Blade,*" I said. "I can't kill a story I'm told to write. If I don't write it, someone else will."

"What the hell kind of story can you write?"

"That's what I asked Mac," I said. "He wants human interest. Atmosphere story on a morgue with a couple of gangsters waiting for a double funeral."

"Where's a story in that?"

"If you stop me, it might make one."

He frowned, and then grinned sourly. He said, "Go ahead and waste some lead off your pencil. Come on, boys."

They got into the car, and I went on up and rang the night bell of the mortuary.

Saul Mintner came and let me in. Saul's the night-duty man at Morris' place. He's a tall, sober-looking guy whom nature obviously designed for an undertaker. You'd hardly class him as human unless you got in a cribbage game with him. He's maybe the best cribbage player in town.

I said, "Hi, Saul. How are the two boy friends?"

"Huh?"

"Monk Rogge and Pete Wendorf. I have to interview them, if you haven't screwed down the lids on their coffins. Let's go in the office first, though."

We did and Saul sat down on the other side of Morris' desk and got out the cards and cribbage board. I wavered, but I said, "O.K. But the story first. I really have to get one, even if it never sees print."

He looked at me with a puzzled look and said, "Slim, are you drunk?"

I grinned. "No, but it's an idea." I had a pint bottle in my pocket that was mostly full, and I took it out and made Saul take a snifter. I had one myself, and it sort of took the taste of Augie out of my mouth and made me feel human again.

"Look, Saul," I said. "The idea is to get some kind of a story to keep the ball rolling till the funeral. If nothing else, this joint's got atmosphere."

"Where?" asked Saul.

"You wouldn't know," I told him. "What were Augie and the boys doing here? All right, go ahead and deal while you tell me."

"Nothing," he said while he shuffled. "Wheeler just wanted to talk about arrangements for the funeral, that's all. He told me a lot of stuff to tell the boss, about tomorrow."

I picked up my hand and discarded cut for the turnover, then asked, "What kind of stuff?"

"What music he wanted, how to place the biers, who was going to be the pallbearers."

"Who?"

"Well, Augie himself and the two that came with him—he said their names were Jeppert and Morrelli—and a guy named Willers, and—"

I whistled softly as I put a six on his nine and pegged two points. "Jim-Jam Willers is the full handle, Saul," I told him. "And I bet I can name the other two—Morgan and Wilento."

"That's right. How did you—"

"Elementary, my dear Saul," I told him. "Willers is Augie's crooked lawyer, and the other four besides Augie himself are the cream of the underworld. Augie's gang, in short. With the dead Monk Rogge and Pete Wendorf, Saul, they made up the eight worst characters that ever ran a crime-ridden town. And tomorrow six of them will carry the other two. Say—won't they need pallbearers? Six to a coffin?"

Saul shook his head. He looked down at his cards. "Fifteen four and a run is seven. No, they'll carry one coffin at a time. But they'll have two hearses and two biers and —"

"Got it!" I said. "The appropriate song for this funeral, Saul. 'Two Biers For Two.' "

Saul looked puzzled. "Why?" he asked. "That gang never peddled beer, did they? They're post-prohibition. They never drank beer, I bet. Alky and probably dope, and probably everything else, but not —"

"Skip it," I told him. You can't explain a joke to Saul. "Yeah, everything else. I'll bet my last buck that Augie is behind that counterfeiting flurry that had the Federal men combing this town last month. He's starting to take over numbers, and I'll give you three guesses who runs the football pools."

"Thirty-one for two," said Saul, playing a seven spot I'd been sure he didn't have. Then: "What I can't see is why the police can't get them."

"There'll come a day," I told him. "Sometime. But Augie Wheeler, damn him, is a smooth duck, my friend. It's one thing to know what his gang does and another to prove it. What this town needs isn't more cops, it's more drunken drivers."

"Huh? Oh, I get you. Maybe they might run into other members of the gang. But suppose they ran into somebody innocent instead? How could you be sure they'd —"

"Skip it," I interrupted. "Sixteen holes for a double-double. How do the corpses look?"

"Not so hot. Identifiable and all that, but pretty messed up. That car that hit theirs must have been traveling plenty fast."

"About sixty," I said. "And Wheeler's boys were going maybe forty themselves. You add that, because they hit head-on, and you get a hundred miles an hour. That's faster than a turtle can crawl; I'm surprised they didn't pick them up with a blotter."

"Not that bad," said Saul. "But they aren't opening the coffins.

We didn't even fix them up for show. Just enough work to—er—preserve them. Want a look?"

"No, thanks. I saw them at the morgue. If you didn't improve them, I—"

The phone on the desk rang, and Saul picked it up. He said, "Yeah, he's here," and handed it across the desk to me.

"Slim?" It was Mac's voice, and he sounded worried. "Listen, you can lay off that story. We decided—"

"Yeah," I said, "Augie Wheeler called you and put on the screws. O.K., you don't have to print it, but I'm going to—"

"Wait, Slim. That isn't the worst. I got a call from—well, from a higher-up, and he says you're through. You won't have to come back tonight unless maybe you want to get your stuff out of your desk."

I didn't say anything. He waited a moment, and then said, "I'm sorry, Slim. It isn't my idea."

"O.K., Mac. It isn't your fault. Listen—"

"What?"

"I—oh, skip it. So long." I hung the receiver back on the hook and stood up.

Saul looked up at me curiously, "Bounced?"

"For talking back to Augie," I told him dully.

"The hell," said Saul. "What are you going to do?"

"What can *I* do," I asked bitterly, "if the whole police department can't pin anything on him?"

"I didn't mean that. You'd be a fool to try. I mean—can you get on another paper here?"

"I don't know." I sat down slowly. I had a hunch that I *did* know. I had a hunch that under the circumstances I'd be too hot for any other local paper to handle.

I said, "Go ahead and deal. Might as well finish this game. Say—why did Augie bring those torpedoes tonight?"

Saul shrugged. "He said that because they were pallbearers,

they wanted to look over the layout. They were looking around out there while Augie Wheeler talked to me in here."

"Sounds like they expect trouble tomorrow," I said thoughtfully. "How long were they here?"

"About half an hour."

"You mean Augie kept you in here *that* long while Morrelli and Jeppert —"

He nodded, and I picked up my hand thoughtfully and stared at the cards without seeing them. What had Augie's men found to do that took them half an hour out in the main funeral parlor?

Well, as soon as this game was over I'd have a look out there myself. I forced myself to concentrate on the cards and put two of them in the crib. The cut turned up a king.

I said, "O.K., Saul, it's your —"

Saul cut in in a different voice, "Don't move your hands, Slim."

I looked up at Saul, and his eyes were staring past me over my shoulder.

A voice behind me said, "And don't turn around!"

There was something vaguely familiar about that voice. I was sure I'd heard it before a long time ago. It wasn't the voice of any of Augie Wheeler's men.

I kept my hands on the desk. I said, "So I won't turn around. And then what?"

The voice said, "Who are— Hell, it's Slim Miller! What you doing here?"

"I *was* after an interview with two guys named Monk and Pete," I said. "As to what I'm doing now—you tell me."

The door closed softly. The voice said, "I'm thinking that over, pal."

I said, "Saul, the gentleman behind me talks as though he has a gun pointed our way. Has he?"

"Yes," said Saul. And the puzzled look in Saul's eyes began to change. He'd been a little scared before, and now he looked like he was a lot scared. And there wasn't any movement behind me, so I guessed it was because Saul had suddenly recognized or remembered who our visitor was.

That meant it wasn't someone Saul knew well or personally. Maybe someone whose picture he'd seen in the newspapers. And it was someone who knew my name, whose voice was familiar to me, although I hadn't heard it for a long time.

Then I placed that voice, with the rest of it as a clue.

Frankie Sorrent!

A little chill started at the base of my spine and went all the way up to the back of my neck. What was Frankie Sorrent, the guy Augie Wheeler had run out of town, doing here tonight?

Could he have been concerned in the deaths of Rogge and Wendorf? No, definitely and positively, the two Wheeler henchmen had died accidentally. There wasn't the faintest possibility of foul play. There'd been plenty of witnesses to the fatal accident, and the man who'd driven head-on into their car had been a respectable, if drunken, citizen. He'd been killed, too.

And then I remembered something else. Frankie Sorrent couldn't be behind me. When Little Augie had taken over the rackets, he'd seen that Frankie wouldn't object; anyway, the people in the know had said that Augie had seen to it. Frankie Sorrent had gone up the river; he'd gone for two twenties and a ten, and the sentences were to run consecutively and not concurrently. That had been four years ago. So it couldn't be Frankie Sorrent standing behind me.

But the voice, and Saul Mintner's eyes, told me that it was Sorrent.

I took a deep breath and let it out slowly, and I forgot that I'd just been fired off the *Blade*. This was a *story* — if I lived to phone it in!

The telephone was to my right on the desk, and Frankie was, judging from where I'd heard his voice, behind me and to the left. I quickly calculated the angle and decided there might be a chance to get my hand under the receiver and lift it half an inch without his seeing me. Then, if I talked loudly enough, and figured my wording so he'd think I was talking to him, maybe the operator would get the idea and send help.

But I was still inches away when Frankie's voice said, "Don't get any ideas," and I knew he'd stepped forward and could see down over my shoulder. He said, "You might as well turn around, Slim. Maybe you recognized my voice, and if you didn't, it don't matter."

I turned around. I moved carefully, because Frankie Sorrent was a killer. He'd spotted my play at the telephone, and his voice had been altogether too calm and quiet when he'd warned me.

I turned slowly and looked at him. He caught the expression in my eyes and said, "Yeah, it's me."

Four years in prison had done to Frankie Sorrent what forty years might do to another man. He was not exactly old in years, but old in the sense that you could tell from looking at him that he wasn't going to live much longer. His face was drawn and the skin looked like dirty parchment across his sharp nose. Those mean, murderous little eyes of his were countersunk into their sockets, but they still burned as I remember they did that last day in court when the judge piled those sentences on him. They'd burned their way, it seemed, half an inch deeper into his skull since then.

Prison does that to a few men. The wildest and fiercest of them. They won't fall into routine and let themselves ride with the current. They buck it, physically and mentally, and it breaks them. It had broken Sorrent — his body, anyway.

He looked like a walking corpse, all but his eyes.

I said, "You escaped, Frankie?" He didn't answer, but the answer was obvious. I asked, "Why'd you come *here?*"

He made a noise that was probably intended for a laugh. "To have fun, Slim."

"How? What's fun in an undertaker's joint?"

He chuckled. "Ever see a jack-in-the-box?"

I didn't answer right away. I thought he was clean off his rocker, and I was trying to think of something to stall him along until I could figure how to handle him. He must have seen what I was thinking, for he said, "I'm not crazy. Not even stir-crazy. What does a jack-in-the-box do?"

"Uh — it jumps up."

He nodded. "And scares hell out of people. That's the idea. That's what I'm going to do. Only with a Tommy-gun in my hands."

I said, "I don't —" and stopped, because maybe I did get what he meant. I whistled softly.

He said, "That's it! Slim, think what their faces will look like when I pop up shooting."

His shoulders shook. "They'll go down like ninepins, Slim. Too bad you won't be able to see it."

Again there was that chill down my spine, and this time it was a colder one. I asked, "Why can't I see it, Frankie? I'll give you a good press on it. And Augie's mob aren't buddies of mine."

He didn't answer. His shoulders were shaking again, and it wasn't murderous mirth; it looked like ague. The muzzle of the gun shook, too, but not enough. Not enough for me to have more than a thousand-to-one chance on a break.

I figured I could do better by talking. I said, "Sit down, Frankie. There's a chair. Want a drink? I got one."

I jerked my thumb toward the pint bottle that I'd put on the desk after Saul and I had drunk out of it. There was still half of it left.

He said, "Yeah — wait," and stood there until the shaking had stopped. Then he said, "Swivel that chair around, Slim. I'll get it. I'm not taking any chances. Not after I've come this far."

I turned around and heard him come toward me; then the

muzzle of the gun was right in the middle of my back while he reached over my shoulder and picked up the bottle. Frankie Sorrent, sane or crazy, still knew his way around.

His feet shuffled back, and I waited seconds before I swiveled around to face him again. He was sitting down in the chair on the other side of the office, and he was tilting the bottle up to drink. But he held his head sidewise to do it, so he could keep one eye on Saul and me.

When he put the bottle down I asked, "How'd you get this far, Frankie?"

He said, "Hell, hasn't the story come through? I shot my way out hours ago. Me and another guy—he got a bellyful of buck-shot—killed a couple guards. So what've I got to lose by bumping Augie and the boys?"

I said, "Your life, maybe. Suppose you get away with hiding in one of those coffins. Suppose you come up shooting when the pallbearers are all here. What chance have you got for a getaway?"

He said, "That's the first good drink I've had in four years."

"What chance have you got for a getaway?"

His eyes burned into mine. He said, "I got a Tommy-gun ready, pal. Knew where to get it. So maybe it's a long chance on a getaway, but I took a long chance to bust out of stir, didn't I? And here I am. The dope on this funeral came in on the grapevine and—" He chuckled. "Know what a jack-in-the-box is, Slim?"

He *was* crazy, yes. You could tell it by his eyes. But you couldn't tell it by the way he held that gun.

And his idea was crazy enough to work—if he really had a Tommy-gun. There'd be a hunt on for him, but who'd think to look in Monk Rogge's or Pete Wendorf's coffin?

The Wheeler mob would know by tomorrow that he was on the loose, and they'd be heeled. But if Frankie picked the right moment to pop up with a machine gun talking, he could mow them down before they could start returning the lead.

Yes, it was crazy enough to work and to have even an off-chance of a getaway afterward. And the odds of that weren't worrying him; his hatred for Augie's mob had been rotting his mind for four years, and he was kill-crazy now.

There was one major trouble with his idea, though, from anybody's point of view but Frankie's. Bullets from a machine gun don't care whom they kill, and at least a few people besides those six pallbearers would stop lead! Maybe quite a few. You can't swing a Tommy-gun at a crowded funeral and be selective about it.

But I didn't bring that up. It wouldn't matter to Frankie and it would show him that I wasn't sympathetic with his idea. Dead, I couldn't stop him. If I stayed alive, there might be a chance sooner or later, for the sake of the innocent people who'd be killed — not for Augie Wheeler. I'd take that chance.

I said, "You and one of those bodies are going to be a bit crowded in a coffin, Frankie."

"I'll get rid of one body." His eyes went past me to Saul. He said, "You keep any spare coffins around, buddy?"

Saul didn't answer right away, and Frankie's eyes narrowed. He said, "I can look myself. But I'll have to shoot you guys first. Might as well talk."

Saul's voice sounded scared and brittle. "Yes, we keep five or six stock models on hand. The cheaper ones."

"Where?"

"Room down in the basement that used to be the morgue when we had only part of this building."

"Where are Monk and Pete?"

"Their coffins are in the main hall, on the biers. We haven't put the flowers on yet."

"Lids fastened down?"

"Just a minute," I cut in, before Saul could answer. "Before we get too cooperative, Frankie, what happens to us? If you're going to kill us anyway, what's the use of our helping you?"

He looked from Saul to me. "All right, see if you can talk your way out of it. But don't look for me to trust you."

I said, "Look, you could tie us up and put us where we wouldn't be found till it's over with."

"Hm-m-m," said Frankie thoughtfully. He looked at Saul. "That room with the spare coffins downstairs—anybody ever go there?"

"Not often," Saul told him. "They won't tomorrow. It's got a door like an icebox, and it's way off from everything else. Even if we got loose or yelled, we wouldn't be heard."

Frankie took another swig out of my bottle and dropped it into his pocket. Then he stood up. "Come on, then. You guys can help move one of the—Hey, wait!" He looked first at Saul and then at me. "Aren't you guys going to be missed?"

"Not me," I said, and I told him why. I figured it wouldn't hurt our chances any to let him know that I had no reason to love Augie Wheeler.

"O.K.," he said, and turned to Saul. "You?"

Saul wet his lips. "Well, I leave at eight o'clock in the morning, and it's all right for me to leave then, whether the day men are here or not. If I'm gone, they'll think I just left, I guess."

Frankie Sorrent looked up at the clock on the wall and said, "Move that about twenty minutes fast. Then, if they get here a little before eight, they'll think it went wrong and that you left according to it."

Saul moved the hands of the clock while I, at Frankie's orders, put the cards and cribbage board in a drawer. If there'd been a gun in the drawer, I'd have tried a break, but there wasn't.

I'd have tried a break because that business about the clock showed me something; it showed me that Frankie might be as crazy as a bedbug when it came to taking a wild chance to get revenge against Augie's mob, but he was still smart enough to figure the little angles.

And leaving Saul and me alive was one of those little angles. Little, I mean to Frankie. It would be safer for him to leave us in that room downstairs dead instead of alive. Alive, there'd always be a chance that we'd figure a way to get out.

But with Frankie keeping the gun on us, we went into the hallway that led back to the main parlor. He had the Tommy-gun, all right; he'd left it just outside the office door. He picked it up, then put the pistol back in his pocket.

We got to the main hall, and Frankie pointed to the coffin on the left. It turned out to be Monk Rogge's.

Saul loosened the four screws that held down the lid, and he and I got the body out. It wasn't hard to tell why they weren't going to have those coffins opened for the funeral. I'd seen Monk at the morgue, and he hadn't improved any in looks since then.

Frankie stood well back, with the Tommy-gun ready. He told us to put the body down and he threw me a hacksaw blade and made me saw off the screws so the heads would show and make the lid look as if it was still screwed down.

That made it all right for Frankie to get in, when it got near morning, and be ready. It was almost five o'clock now and getting gray outside. He had a couple of hours yet to spare before he'd have to hide.

When I'd finished with the screws so the lid would open freely, he said, "Pick up the stiff and get going."

Saul and I carried what was left of Monk Rogge down the back stairs to a vaultlike room off to one side of a long dark hallway. There were six new coffins in the room; we put Monk into one of them.

Frankie said, "O.K., you two. Get in a couple of them your-selves."

I stared at him. "Get in? Without tying us? If you screw down the lids, we'll suffocate!"

"Enough air gets through the cloth and around the edges. Get in!"

He kept both hands on the Tommy-gun, and the muzzle was aimed right at me from ten feet away. He couldn't have missed with that thing; the first burst would have cut me in half!

If there'd been a chance in a million for a break, I'd have taken it. I was sorry that I hadn't taken a chance in a thousand and jumped him in the office while he had only the pistol. I didn't believe now that he was going to let us live. I had an awful hunch why he was making us get into coffins: not so he could screw down the lids, but so our bodies would be neatly put away out of sight.

I caught a glimpse of Saul's face as he started to get into one of the coffins. He was to one side, but he was as far away from Frankie Sorrent as I was. Frankie was watching me, mostly; and as I opened the lid of a coffin I saw what Saul was doing, and kept from looking that way on the chance that Frankie wouldn't notice. Saul was getting into the coffin backward — with his feet at the head. It gave him an outside chance. Frankie's eyes were on me, and I hesitated to hold his attention. He said, "Hurry up or —" He took a couple of steps, not toward me, but back toward the doorway.

My hunch was that he was going to shoot us through the coffins! But there wasn't any way to play that hunch; I could only hope that it was wrong.

Frankie snapped, "Put down the lid," and I put it down. It's dark and not pleasant inside a coffin, despite the padding, when you're lying there waiting for a machine gun to talk.

It began to talk! In the confined space of that room it sounded like a revolution in hell. It went on for what seemed hours, but was probably only a second or two. Then there was deafening silence.

A door slammed and a bolt slid home.

I was still alive.

Or was I? It didn't make sense if I was. But I found I could

move, and I pushed up the lid of the coffin. It was as dark outside
the coffin as it had been inside. I'd have been scared by that utter
blackness if there'd been any scare left in me, but there wasn't.

For a minute I didn't wonder *why* I was still alive; I just took
it for granted and held my wondering for later. But Saul? I called
his name softly.

There was a muffled groan and a sound that might have been
my name. I groped through darkness thick as ink until I found
the coffin I'd seen him getting into; then I raised the lid.

"Saul, you all right?" I remembered matches in my pocket and
groped for them.

Saul said, "Just my legs. Damn —"

I got a match going. Saul's face, in its flare, was gray with
pain and the legs of his trousers were bloody halfway up the thigh.
He didn't seem hit anywhere else that I could see. The vertical
row of bullet holes on the outside of the coffin showed that the
slugs would have gone through his chest if he'd got into the coffin
the right way.

I said, "Are there lights I can turn on from in here?"

He nodded. "The door — circuit breaker when door closes.
Lights go on automatically when it opens. How come you got by?"

I took a look around before the flame of the match died, and
located the door. Then, in darkness, I groped toward it. I said,
"Wait till I get lights. Maybe he shot at your coffin first and then
made a mistake and shot up the wrong one for me."

Then my hands found the door. I felt along the edge of the
door until I came to a little metal box screwed on the edge of
the jamb. A minute later the lights went on again as I pressed
the catch and wedged it in with a toothpick.

I went back to Saul, slit his trousers leg with my penknife and
did what I could for his wounds. He'd taken four bullets out of
twelve or so that had gone through the coffin. All the bullets had
gone clean through, and all I could do was stop most of the
bleeding and put on rough bandages.

I said, "I think you better not take a chance on moving till we get a doc. I don't think a bone has been hit, but there's no use of taking a chance on moving. Is there any way I can get out of here to bring help?"

Saul had gotten over the shock. He was in pain, but he talked more easily. He said, "No dice. I wasn't kidding Sorrent. This room's like an icebox, door and all. We'll have to wait till they find us."

"How about ventilation?"

He pointed to a pair of small gratings in opposite corners. "Intake and outlet. Goes to outside; fan somewhere in between."

"Maybe if I yelled into it —" I started across toward the outlet grating; but Saul called, "Hey, wait! Frankie'll be the first to hear." And anyway, if that Tommy-gun hadn't attracted attention outside, my yelling wouldn't.

"We'll have to wait until well after eight o'clock," Saul pointed out. "After he's hidden in Rogge's coffin, he won't hear, and the others might."

It was a long three hours until eight o'clock. After I'd looked at the coffin that had nearly been *my* coffin, and figured why it wasn't, we played cribbage. Saul said having something to do would keep his mind off the pain. I made cards from half leaves of a notebook and marked out a cribbage board with squares on the floor beside the coffin Saul was in. We used pennies in lieu of pegs.

At a quarter to eight I said, "Frankie will be hiding in the coffin by now. I'm going to —"

"No," said Saul. "Wait till we're sure somebody else'll be up there. Wait till eight fifteen."

"But —"

"Wait! My legs are numb, anyway."

I could see by his face that he was lying, but I waited until five minutes past eight.

Then I went over to the grating and started to yell.

Nothing happened.

For over half an hour, nothing happened except that I was hoarse and my throat felt raw. I'd hammered on the grating, too, with everything I could find suitable for hammering.

And then it was ten minutes to nine, and nothing had happened. In ten minutes the funeral would start.

It took me that long, forty-five minutes, to get a better idea than making noise. But once I got it, I worked fast. I tore the lining from a coffin, pulled out big handfuls of the kapok padding and piled it under the outlet grating.

Then I touched a match to it and held my coat in a tent over it to send as much of the smoke as possible into the grating.

Even with the coat, we were nearly choked with smoke by the time the police, looking for the fire, got around to opening the door of the room we were in.

Luckily, Lieutenant Barr was with them. I gave him the dope, and we were on our way upstairs while the other cops were carrying Saul out. The coffin he was in made a better stretcher than a stretcher does. Later, when I went to see him at the hospital and learned his legs would be all right, he was still grinning over the shock it gave the hospital attendants to have him brought in that way.

The six pallbearers were all there—Augie Wheeler and his gang. Augie's eyes went wide, and then narrow, as he saw me walk in, coatless and sooty, with Lieutenant Barr. Augie and his men were standing together at one side of the room—a perfect set-up for Frankie Sorrent. But Frankie hadn't popped up yet.

Barr and I tiptoed to the coffin that had been Monk Rogge's and, as I yanked up the lid, Barr grabbed the Tommy-gun from the surprised Frankie before he could get his finger on the trigger.

And that was that—for Frankie Sorrent. Two policemen who had come in right after us grabbed him.

Barr pointed the Tommy-gun at Little Augie and those around him. He said, "Stand still, boys, we'll collect your hardware in a minute."

Augie Wheeler looked more puzzled than scared. He looked from Barr to me and said, "What the hell are you guys talking about?"

I grinned at him. I said, "Thanks for saving my life, Augie, even if you didn't mean it. Those plates for the counterfeit money you got rid of last night by stashing them in the lining of a couple of spare coffins that would soon be six feet out of sight made swell armor plate. But the Federal men will make more than that out of them."

Other cops were taking over, and I ran for a phone and got the city editor. He said, "Mac told me he had to fire—"

"Shut up and listen," I cut in, and gave it to him:

"Augie found those plates too hot when the Federal men got nosing around. He came here probably with the idea of hiding them in Monk's or Pete's coffin and getting rid of them. He kept Saul busy in the office while Morrelli and Jeppert hid the plates. They found there were spare coffins and that was a better bet than ones of members of the gang, even if they wouldn't be buried right away, see? They never thought the plates would come to light, and they weren't— Yeah, fingerprints; the government can get an air-tight case. They were copper plates, backed type high with lead for use on a hand press. Frankie's Tommy-gun messed some of them up, but—"

"Swell," he said. "That's worth an extra. I'll give you a rewrite man; then come on around and bat out a three-column eyewitness for the regular edition."

"With a by-line?"

"Naturally, you dope. What's the—"

"How can I, if I don't work there any more?"

And I chuckled while he got the cussing out of his system and calmed himself down enough to switch me to a rewrite man.

SEE NO MURDER

Even reading about it in the papers gave me a mild case of the willies. For some reason I had a hunch, right off, that I was going to be put on the case and that I wasn't going to like it. Of course they might have it cleaned up by the time I got back—it was the next to last day of my vacation—but I didn't think so.

I put down the paper and tried to forget what I'd read by looking at Marge. Even after four years of being married, I like to look at Marge.

But this time it didn't drive what I'd been reading out of my head. By a roundabout way, it brought me back to it. I got to thinking how bad it would be to be blind and never able to see Marge again. The story in the paper had been about a blind man—a blind man who was the only witness to a murder.

Marge happened to look up; she asked me what I was thinking about and I told her. She was interested, so I told her the details—what there was in the paper.

"The blind man's name is Max Easter. Until three days ago he was the bookkeeper at the Springfield Chemical Works. Until three days ago he wasn't blind—and they're not sure now whether his blindness is permanent; it's from an industrial accident at the plant. Some acid splashing in his face while he was collecting time slips out in the plant. They think he'll recover; but right now he's completely blind, and with his eyes bandaged.

"So yesterday evening he was in his bedroom — he's still in bed — talking to a friend of his named Armin Robinson, who'd dropped in to see him. Their wives — Easter's and Robinson's — had gone to a movie together, downtown. The two men were alone in the house — except for whoever killed one of them.

"Armin Robinson was sitting in a chair near the bed, and the bedroom door was ajar. Max Easter was sitting up in bed and the two of them were talking. Then Easter heard the door squeak and someone step into the room. He heard Robinson move and thinks he may have stood up, but nothing was said. Then all of a sudden there was a shot and the sound of a fall, from Robinson's direction. And then the footsteps came farther into the room and Easter sat there in bed, waiting to be shot, too."

Marge said, "How awful."

I said, "Then comes the odd part. Instead of being shot, Max Easter feels something land on the bed, on the mattress. He gropes for it and he's got a gun in his hand, a revolver. Then he hears the killer move and points the gun in that direction and pulls the trigger —"

"You mean the killer gave him the gun? Tossed it on his bed, I mean? Wouldn't he have known that even a blind man can shoot at sound?"

I said, "All I know is what's in the papers, Marge. That's the way they tell Easter's story. But it could be. Probably the killer didn't realize that the bounce of the mattress would tell Easter where the gun landed and that he'd get it in his hand that quickly, the first grab. Probably he thought he could be out of the room before Easter would find the gun."

"But why give it to him at all?"

"I don't know. But to go on with Easter's story: As he swings the gun around to aim at the sound, he hears a noise like a man's knee hitting the floor and he figures the killer has dropped down to be under the shot if he fires. So Easter lowers the gun to aim a couple of feet above the floor and pulls the trigger. Just once.

"And then, suddenly, he says, he got more scared of what he was doing than of what might happen to him, and he dropped the gun. He was shooting in the dark — literally. If he'd misjudged what had happened, he might be shooting at Armin Robinson — at anybody. He didn't even know for sure that there'd been a murder, or what had happened.

"So, anyway, he dropped the gun and it hit the edge of the bed and clunked onto the floor. So he couldn't get it back even if he changed his mind. And he just sat there sweating, while whoever it was moved around the room a while and then went out."

Marge looked thoughtful. "Moved around the room doing what, George?"

"How would Easter know? But Armin Robinson's wallet was gone, so taking it was probably one thing. And Easter's own wallet and watch were gone off the dresser, where his wife said later they'd been lying. And a small suitcase was gone."

"A suitcase? Why would he take a suitcase?"

"To put the silverware in. That was gone from downstairs and a few other minor articles a burglar might take along. Easter says the man moved around his room for what seemed a long time, but was probably only a minute or two. Then he heard him walk down the stairs and move around a while down there, and then the back door opened and closed, and the house was quiet.

"He hadn't dared get up until he heard the killer leave the house. Then he groped his way to Robinson and found he was dead. So he felt his way down the stairs to the telephone and called police. Period. End of story."

"But that's horrible," Marge said. "I mean, it leaves so many loose ends, so many things you can wonder about."

"Which is just what I've been doing. Particularly, I get the picture of that blind man shooting in the dark and then getting scared because he didn't know what he was shooting at."

"George, don't blind people get special senses? I mean, so they can tell who a person is by the way he walks — things like that?"

Very patiently I said, "Max Easter had been blind all of two days. He might have been able to tell a man's walk from a woman's — if a woman wore high heels."

"I guess you're right. Even if he'd known the man —"

I said, "Even if it had been a friend of his, he wouldn't have known. At night, all cats are grey."

"All cats *be* grey."

"You're goofy," I said.

"Look it up."

Marge and I are always quibbling over things like that. I got Bartlett's out of the bookcase and looked it up and this time she was right. I'd been wrong on the "at night" part, too; it read "When all candles be out, all cats be grey."

When I'd admitted to Marge that she was right — for a change — and we'd batted that around for a while, her mind went back to the murder again. She said, "What about the gun he left, George? Can they trace him from it? The serial number, or something?"

I said, "It was Max Easter's own gun. It was in the drawer of a desk downstairs. I forgot to mention that. The killer must have rifled that desk before he came upstairs."

"Do you think, George, that it was just a burglar?"

"No," I told her.

"Neither do I. There's something about it — a false note."

"More than a false note. A whole damn discord. But I can't guess what it is."

She said, "This Max Easter. Maybe he isn't blind at all."

I snorted at that. "Woman's intuition! A guess like that is as silly—unless you've got a reason for saying it—as saying that what he shot at was a grey cat, just because I happened to mention the proverb about one."

"Maybe he did," Marge said.

That wasn't even worth answering. I picked up the paper again and turned to the sports section.

The Sunday papers, the next day, had a lot on the case, but none of it was new. No arrests had been made, and apparently no one was even under suspicion. I hoped I wouldn't get put on it. I don't know why, exactly. I just hoped so.

I was on it almost before I got inside the door. Before I got my raincoat off, I was told Captain Eberhart wanted me in his office, and I went in.

"Have a good vacation, George?" he asked me, but he didn't wait for my answer. He went on: "I'm putting you on that Armin Robinson murder. Have you read about it in the papers?"

"Sure," I said.

"Then you know as much about it as anybody else, except one thing. I'll tell you that, but outside of that, I want you to go on it cold, without any preconceived ideas. We haven't got anywhere and you just might hit something we missed. It's worth a try."

I nodded. "But how about lab reports, ballistics? I can tackle the people cold, but I'd like to have all the physical facts."

"Okay. The coroner's report is that Robinson died instantaneously from a bullet through his head. The bullet was in the wall about three feet behind where he'd been sitting and about five and a half feet up from the floor. Went into the wall almost straight. It all checks if he stood up when the killer came through the door and if he stood in the doorway or just inside to fire the shot and held the gun at eye level."

"Bullet matches the gun?"

"Yes, and so does the other bullet, the one Max Easter fired. And there were two empty shells in the gun. No prints on the gun besides Easter's; the killer must have worn gloves. And Mrs. Easter says a pair of white cotton work gloves is missing from the kitchen."

"Any way Max Easter could have fired both shots instead of just one?"

"Absolutely not, George. He is blind—at least temporarily. The doctor treating him guarantees that. There are tests—reaction of pupils to sudden light, things like that. The only way a blind man could hit someone dead center in the forehead would be to hold the gun against him—and there weren't any powder burns. No, Max Easter's story sounds screwy, but all the facts fit it. Even the timing. Some neighbors heard the shots, thought they were backfires and didn't investigate. But they noticed the time—they were listening to the radio and it was at the eight o'clock change of programs—two shots about five seconds apart. And Easter's phone call to us was at twelve minutes after eight by our own records. Twelve minutes just about fits what he says went on between the shooting and his getting to the phone."

"How about the alibis of the two wives?"

"Good as gold. They were together in a movie at the time of the murder. Eight o'clock was just about the time they were going in, in fact, and they saw friends in the lobby, so it's not only their own word. You can take the alibi as okay."

"All right," I said, "and what's the one thing that didn't get in the papers?"

"Lab report on the other bullet, the one Easter fired at the murderer, shows traces of organic matter."

I whistled. "Then the killer was wounded?" That ought to make it a lot easier.

Cap Eberhart said, "Maybe." He sighed. "I almost hate to tell you this, George, but if he was, he was a rooster wearing silk pajamas."

"That's fine," I told him. "My wife says Easter was shooting at a grey cat, and my wife is mostly right. About everything. But now would you mind talking sense?"

"If you can make sense out of it, swell. We dug the second bullet out of the wall near the door, about a foot and a half up. The microscopist who examined it says there are minute traces of three kinds of organic matter on it. Infinitesimal quantities — he can identify them only up to a point. But he thinks they're blood, silk and feathers. A chicken wearing silk pajamas would be one answer."

"What kind of blood?" I asked. "What kind of feathers?"

"No dice. They're minute traces, and he won't stick his neck out any farther than that, even on a guess. What's this business about a grey cat?"

I told him about our argument over the quotation and Marge's kidding remark.

I said, "Seriously, Cap, it does sound as though the killer were wounded. Just a scrape, probably, since he went about his business afterwards. That takes care of the blood on the bullet, and the silk isn't too hard. Silk shirt, silk shorts, silk tie — anything. But the feathers are harder to figure. Only place a man's likely to wear a feather is in the band of a new hat."

Eberhart nodded. "Pajama-wearing roosters aside, that's the best suggestion we've had to date. Could be like this — the killer sees the gun swinging toward him and drops down low, throwing up his hand toward the gun. Hands don't stop bullets, but people often do that when they're going to be shot at. The bullet grazes his hand, grazes his hat band, which is silk and has a feather in it — but not hard enough to crease him or stun him — and goes in the wall. Then the killer wraps a handkerchief around his hand and goes about his business, after Easter drops the gun off the bed and he sees he's safe."

"It could be," I said. "Anybody connected with the case wounded?"

"Not where it shows. And we haven't got enough on anybody to drag them in and strip them. In fact, dammit, we haven't even found anybody with a motive. Screwy as it seems, George, we've almost decided that it really was a plain and simple robbery. Well, that's all I'm going to tell you. Go at it cold and maybe you'll get something we missed."

I put my raincoat back on and went out.

Chapter Two: Murder Without Motive

The first thing to do was the thing I hated worst—talk to the widow of the murdered man. I hoped, for both our sakes, that she'd be over the worst part of the shock and grief.

I didn't enjoy it, but it wasn't as bad as it could have been. Mrs. Armin Robinson was quiet and reserved, but she was willing to talk, and able to talk unemotionally. The emotion was there, but it was two layers down; it wasn't going to come to the surface in hysteria.

I got the matter of her alibi over first. Yes, she and Mrs. Max Easter, the blinded man's wife, had met at eight o'clock in the theater lobby. She was sure it was eight exactly, because both she and Louise Easter had commented on the fact that they were both exactly on time; Louise had been there first, but had said she'd been waiting less than a minute. Louise had been talking to two friends of theirs whom she'd met—accidentally, not by appointment—in the lobby. The four women had gone in together and had stayed together in the movie. She gave me the names of the two other women, and their addresses. It sounded, as Eberhart had said, as good as gold. The theater they'd gone to was at least twenty minutes' driving time from the Easter residence, where the murder had occurred.

I asked, "Did your husband have any enemies?"

"No, definitely not. Possibly a few people may have disliked him, but no more than that."

I asked gently, "Why would some people have disliked him, Mrs. Robinson?"

"He was pretty much of an extrovert. You know, the life of the party, that sort of thing. When he had a few drinks, he may have grated on some people's nerves. But that didn't happen often. And, too, some people thought him a little too frank. But those were little things."

They certainly didn't sound like something that would lead to premeditated murder. I said, "He was a C.P.A., an auditor. Is that right?"

"Yes, and he operated independently. He was his own boss."

"Any employes?"

"Only a secretary, full time. He had a list of people he sometimes called on for help in an audit that was too big a job for one man."

"How close friends were you and your husband with the Easters?"

"Fairly close. Probably Armin and Max were closer friends than Louise and I are. Frankly, I don't like Louise too well, but I got along with her because of the friendship between my husband and hers. Not that I have anything against Louise — don't misunderstand me — it's just that we're such different types. For that matter, I don't think Armin liked Louise especially either."

"How often did you see them?"

"Sometimes oftener, but at least once a week regularly. We're — we were — members of a bridge club of four couples who took turns meeting at one another's homes."

"Who were the others?"

"The Anthonys and the Eldreds. Bill Anthony is editor of the Springfield Blade. He and his wife are away on vacation right now, in Florida. Lloyd Eldred is with the Springfield Chemical Works — the same company Max Easter works for. He's Max's immediate superior there."

"And Max Easter is bookkeeper there?"

"That's right, bookkeeper and paymaster. Lloyd Eldred is the treasurer of the company. That's probably not as much of a difference as it sounds. I think Max probably makes about five thousand a year and Lloyd about seven thousand. Springfield Chemical doesn't pay very high salaries to its officers."

"Your husband ever do any auditing for Springfield Chemical?"

"No. Kramer and Wright have done their auditing for years. I think Armin could have had the account if he'd gone after it, but he had all the business he could handle by himself."

"He was doing well, then?"

"Well enough. About ten thousand a year."

"This is an unpleasant question, Mrs. Robinson. But does anyone gain by his death?"

"Not unless you'd consider that I did. There's ten thousand in insurance and title to this house is clear. But almost no savings; we bought this house a year ago and used our savings to buy it outright. And Armin's business can't be sold — there's nothing to sell. I mean, he just sold his own services as an auditor."

"Then I wouldn't say you gained," I told her. "Ten thousand in insurance doesn't compensate for the loss of ten thousand a year in income."

"Nor for the loss of a husband, Mr. Hearn."

That could have been corny except that it sounded sincere. It made me remember I wanted to get out of there, so I got down to brass tacks by asking her about Friday evening. "Had your husband planned in advance to go to the Easters'?" I asked. "Would anyone know he was going to be there?"

"No, except Louise and myself. And then, only just before he left. Here's what happened: Louise and I had made the movie date before Max's accident at the plant. About half-past six that evening, when Armin and I were just starting dinner, Louise phoned. She said she'd better not leave Max home alone; that he was feeling pretty low.

"Armin heard my end of the phone conversation and guessed what it was about. So he came to the phone and talked to Louise and said she should keep her date for the movie — that he'd just as soon go over and sit with Max for the evening."

"When did he leave to go there?"

"About seven, because he was going by streetcar and wanted to get there by half-past seven, so Louise would have time to make the date. He told me to take our car and pick him up after the show to bring him back home."

"And he got to the Easters' by half-past seven?"

"Yes. That is, Louise said so. She says he went upstairs right away to Max's room, and that she left about ten minutes after that. She drove their car. We had two cars between the two of us, which wasn't very good planning, I guess."

I asked, "Was there anything unusual about the way your husband acted Friday evening, before he left? Or, for that matter, any time lately?"

"He'd been a bit moody and preoccupied for two or three days. I asked him several times if he was worried about something, but he insisted that he wasn't."

I tried prying a little deeper on that, but couldn't find out whether she had any guess as to what he may have been worrying about. She was sure it wasn't financial troubles.

I let it go at that and left her, telling her I might have to come back later to talk to her again. She was pleasant about that and said she understood.

I thought it over after I got in my car. The alibis of both wives sounded solid. Neither of them could have been at the theater at eight and still have killed Armin Robinson. But I didn't want to take anything for granted, so I drove to the addresses of the two other women who'd seen Louise Easter and Mrs. Robinson in the movie lobby. I talked to both of them and when I left the second, I was sure.

I got back in my car and drove out to the Springfield Chemical Works. I didn't see how Max's accident there — his blinding — could have anything to do with the murder of Robinson, but I wanted to get that angle out of the way before I went to the Easters'.

Springfield Chemical must have had an efficient office system; their office quarters were quite small for a plant that hired over a hundred men.

I asked the receptionist, who was doubling in brass on a type-writer and had a telephone switchboard in front of her, for Mr. Lloyd Eldred. She made a call and then directed me to his office.

I went in. There were two desks, but only one of them was occupied. A tall, slender, almost effeminate-looking man with rumpled curly black hair looked up from the occupied desk and said "Yes?" in a tone that meant, "I hope this won't take long; I'm awfully busy." And from all the stuff stacked on his desk, he was.

I said, "I'm George Hearn, Mr. Eldred. From Homicide." I took the chair in front of his desk.

He ran his fingers through his hair, thereby explaining why it was so rumpled. He said, "About Armin Robinson again, I suppose," and I admitted the fact.

"Well — I don't know what more I can tell you. But Armin was a friend of mine and if there is anything —"

"He was a close friend of yours?"

"Well, not exactly. We saw each other at least once a week, at a bridge club that met around at our houses. The Easters, the Anthonys, the Robinsons, and my wife and I."

I nodded. "Mrs. Robinson told me about that. Are you going to continue the club?"

"I don't know. Maybe we'll find another couple — but not until after Max Easter's eyes are all right again. Right now we'd be missing two couples — three, until the Anthonys get back from Florida."

"You think Easter's eyes will get all right again?"

"I don't see why not. The doctor says they will—he's a little puzzled that they've been bad for this long. We gave him a sample of the acid, and he says it definitely should not cause permanent injury to the eyes."

He ran his fingers through his hair again. "I hope—for selfish reasons if no others—that he's back soon. I'm swamped here trying to handle both our jobs."

"Can't your company get another man?"

"They could, I suppose, and would if I wanted them to. We discussed it, in fact. The catch is it would take weeks to break someone in to the point where they'd be a help instead of a hindrance. And the doctor says he thinks Max should be back in another week at the outside. Anyway, it won't be so bad after Wednesday, day after tomorrow."

"Why Wednesday?" I asked him.

"Semi-monthly payroll. That's Max's main job, keeping payroll and time records. This time I'm having to do them besides my own work, so it'll be tough until the payroll's done. But if Max isn't able to be back by next payroll, we will make other arrangements. I can't work twelve hours a day indefinitely."

I nodded. Apparently the guy really was plugging, and I liked the fact that he gave it to me diplomatically instead of telling me to hurry up and get it over with.

So I asked the one routine question I had to ask about Armin Robinson—whether Lloyd Eldred knew any reason anyone would have for wanting Robinson dead—and got a flat, unequivocal no. Also a no as to whether Eldred knew what Robinson might have been worrying about for a few days before his death; Eldred hadn't noticed that he was as of the last time they'd played bridge together and that was the last time he'd seen him.

So I switched to the other matter. "Will you tell me about Max Easter's accident?"

"Max can tell you about it better than anyone else, because he was alone when it happened. All I know is that he was out in the plant—in the plating room—collecting time slips during the men's lunch hour. He takes a later lunch period himself so he can collect slips while they're off. He can go through the whole plant in an hour that way; it'd take twice as long when there's work going on."

I asked, "But didn't he tell you how it happened?"

"Oh, sure. He went in one of the little vat rooms off the plating room to get a slip off a shelf there, where the man who works that vat always leaves it. When he took down the slip pad he knocked down a jug from the shelf into the vat below it. It's a bad arrangement, having to reach across the vat to get something on the shelf, especially as that shelf is slightly above eye level. We changed the arrangement there since then."

I asked, "Was the acid that blinded him in the jug that fell, or in the vat?"

"In the vat. But landing smack in the middle of the vat, the jug splashed acid all over him."

"Any damage except to his eyes?"

"No, unless you count damage to clothes. Probably ruined the suit he was wearing. But the acid wasn't strong enough to hurt the skin."

"Does the company assume responsibility?"

"Of course. At any rate, he's on full salary and we're taking care of medical expenses."

"But if the injury is permanent?"

"It can't be—we have the assurance of the doctor who's treating him. In fact, he tends to believe that the blindness may be hysterical. You've heard of hysterical blindness, haven't you?"

I said I'd heard of it. "But for something like that there is supposed to be a deep-rooted psychic cause. Would there be in Max's case?"

I thought he hesitated slightly before he said, "Not that I know of."

I paused, trying to think of further questions, and I couldn't. From the way Lloyd Eldred looked at me, he was wondering why I'd been asking so many questions about Max's accident and about Max. I was wondering that, too. And I looked again at the piles of work on his desk and I thanked him and excused myself.

It was nearly noon. I was only ten minutes' drive from home, so I decided to have lunch with Marge. Sometimes I go home for lunch and sometimes not, depending on what part of town I happen to be in when lunch time comes around. Marge always keeps stuff on hand that she can rustle up quickly if I do get home.

Chapter Three: Blind Man's Bluff

"I'm on it," I told her, as soon as I got in. She knew what I meant — I didn't have to tell her.

While we ate I told her the little I'd learned that hadn't been in the papers. I said, "So you see it wasn't a grey cat Max Easter was shooting at in the dark. It was a rooster in silk pajamas. For once you're wrong on a hunch. And on your other wild idea, too — Easter is really blind."

She turned up her nose at me. "Bet you a dime he isn't."

I said, "That's one dime I'll collect."

"Maybe. I won't bet you on the grey cat, but it's no sillier than Captain Eberhart's rooster in pajamas. Or than your silk hatband with a feather in it."

"But if it was that, he'd have worn it out with him. If it was a grey cat, what happened to it?"

"The killer carried it out in the suitcase he took from the closet, naturally."

I threw up my hands on that one.

Just the same, Marge had been serious in regard to her hunch that Max Easter wasn't really blind, and when Marge takes one of her hunches seriously, I do too. At least to the extent of checking as thoroughly as I can. So before I left home I phoned Cap Eberhart and got the name and address of the doctor who was treating Max Easter's eyes.

I went to see him and was lucky enough to get into his office right away. After I'd identified myself and explained what I wanted, I asked him, "How soon after the accident did you see Mr. Easter?"

"I believe I reached the plant not over twenty minutes after I was phoned. And the phone call, I was told, had been made immediately."

"Did you notice anything unusual about the condition of his eyes?"

"Nothing unusual considering the dilute acid that had been splashed into them. I'm not sure I understand your question."

I wasn't sure I understood it myself; I didn't know exactly what I was fishing for. I asked, "Was he in considerable pain?"

"Pain? Oh, no. Tetrianic acid causes temporary blindness, but without pain. It's no more painful than boric acid."

"Can you describe the effect for me, Doctor?"

"It dilutes the pupils, as does belladonna. Ultimately, it's as harmless. But in addition to dilation of the pupils, which is an immediate reaction, it causes temporary paralysis of the optic nerves and consequent temporary blindness. Normally the duration of blindness is from two to eight hours, depending on the strength of the solution."

"And the strength of the solution in this case?"

"Medium. Mr. Easter should have recovered his sight in not over six hours."

"But he didn't," I pointed out.

"He hasn't as yet. And that leads to one of two possible con-clusions. One, that he is abnormal in his lack of tolerance for the substance in question. In that case, it is merely a matter of time; his eyesight will return before much longer. The other possibility is, of course, hysterical blindness — blindness caused by self-delusion. I am almost certain this is not true in Mr. Easter's case. However, if his blindness persists more than a week, I shall recommend a psychiatrist."

I asked, "Isn't there a third possibility? Malingering?"

He smiled. "Don't forget, Mr. Hearn, that I am employed by the company and in the company's interests. He couldn't possibly pretend dilation of the pupils, which still persists. And he is not faking blindness. There are certain tests. And I am, as I said, reasonably sure it is not hysterical. I base that on the continued dilation of the pupils. Hysteria would be much more likely to continue the nerve paralysis alone."

"When did you examine him last?"

"Yesterday afternoon at four. I've been calling every day at that time."

I thanked him and left. For once, one of Marge's hunches had been wrong.

And I'd been stalling long enough on going to the Easters' house. I went there. I rang the doorbell.

A woman who turned out to be Mrs. Max Easter, Louise Easter, opened the door. I identified myself and she identified herself and she asked me in. She was a good-looking woman, even in a house dress. It would have been interesting to examine her to see if she had any bullet scrapes — but then her alibi was as good as any I've ever seen, and besides there's Marge.

Her husband, Louise Easter told me, was still in bed in his room upstairs and did I want to go up? I said I did, but that first she might as well show me around downstairs because I wanted to learn the layout of the place.

She showed me around. The drawer from which Max's gun had been taken, the cabinet where the silverware had been, the shelf in the kitchen where the cotton gloves had lain.

"Those were the only things missing?" I asked.

"Yes. From downstairs, that is. He took Max's wallet and watch from the dresser upstairs. There was about twenty dollars in the wallet, and that's all the money there happened to be in the house. And the suitcase."

"How big a suitcase was it?"

She held her hands to show me — it had been about two feet by one foot by seven inches. Bigger than he'd have needed to carry what he took — but maybe he'd thought he'd find more.

I asked her to tell me just what had happened that evening, starting at the time she phoned Mrs. Armin Robinson to call off the movie date.

She said, "That would have been somewhere around half-past six; I'd just given Max his dinner but hadn't washed the dishes yet. I decided I'd better not go and leave Max alone. But then Armin said he'd come around and talk to Max and that I should go. And by the time I finished the dishes and got dressed, Armin was here. That would have been about half past seven, I guess.

"I didn't have to leave right away to get to the movie by eight — that's when our appointment was — so I stayed and talked with both of them, up in Max's room, for five or ten minutes, and when I left, and that must have been — oh, at least twenty minutes before eight, because I got to the show a minute or two ahead of time and Ianthe — Mrs. Robinson, that is — got there just at eight."

"Did you lock the front door when you left?"

"No. I wondered whether I should and decided not to because it isn't a spring lock. I'd have had to lock it from the outside and take the key and that would have seemed funny, to lock Armin and Max in. The back door was locked though."

"You think the killer got in after you left, between then and eight o'clock?"

"He must have, unless he was hiding in the basement. He couldn't have been upstairs. There are only the two bedrooms, the hall and the bath, and I was in all of them. And he couldn't have been downstairs, because when I came down, ready to leave, I couldn't find my purse right away and had to look for it. I found it in the kitchen, but looked everywhere else first."

I asked, "How are your husband's eyes? Any improvement?"

She shook her head. "I'm afraid not—yet. And I'm getting really worried, in spite of what the doctor says. Up to this morning, anyway, there'd been no improvement at all."

"This morning?"

"When I changed the bandage and bathed them. I'll have to do it again in about an hour. You won't have to talk to him longer than that, will you?"

"Probably not that long," I told her. "But maybe I'd better start now, in that case."

We went up the stairs. The door of one of the bedrooms was ajar, just as it must have been Friday evening. And through it I could see Max Easter, his eyes bandaged, sitting up in a bed. Just as the killer must have seen him when he'd walked up these stairs after Louise Easter had left.

I stood in the doorway where the killer must have stood, first, to fire the shot that killed Armin Robinson, before he'd stepped closer to the bed and tossed down the revolver on the mattress.

Louise Easter had preceded me into the room and said, "Max, this is Mr. Hearn from the Homicide Department," and I was acknowledging the introduction without thinking about it, because I was looking around the room, seeing the chair Armin Robinson must have been sitting on—the one next to the bed— and the hole in the plaster above and behind that chair where the bullet had been dug out of the wall. And I turned and saw the place where the other bullet had been dug out. It was about a foot and a half up from the floor and about five feet from the doorway.

The bullet that Max Easter had fired. The one that had showed minute traces of blood, silk and feathers. Not blood, sweat and tears — but blood, silk and feathers.

I visualized the line of fire — Max sitting up in bed, aiming the gun at a sound, then lowering the muzzle as he heard the killer's knee hit the floor. I tried to visualize the killer standing somewhere in that line of fire, then crouching or kneeling to get under the muzzle of the gun.

But Max Easter had said something to me and I had to think back to the sound of the words to get that he had asked me to sit down.

I said, "Thanks," and crossed over to sit in the chair that Robinson had sat in. I looked toward the door. No, from that angle, Robinson would not have been able to see the head of the stairs. No matter how far ajar the door had been, he couldn't have seen the killer until the man had actually stepped into the room.

I looked from Max Easter to Louise Easter and then around the room, and I realized that I hadn't said anything for some time and that Easter couldn't tell what I was doing.

I said, "I'm just looking around, Mr. Easter, trying to visualize how things must have happened."

He smiled a bit wanly. He said, "Take your time. I've got lots of it. Louise, I'm going to get up a little while; I'm tired of the bed. Will you get my bathrobe?"

"Of course, Max, but —" She didn't go on with the protest, whatever it had been going to be. She got his bathrobe from the closet and held it while he slipped it on over his pajamas. He sat back down on the edge of the bed.

He asked, "Would you like a bottle of beer, Mr. Hearn?"

I opened my mouth to say that I would like one but that I

never drank on duty. Then I realized that he wouldn't be able to get the beer, that Louise would have to go downstairs for it, and that just possibly he had that in mind—that he might want to say something to me privately.

So I said, "Sure, thanks."

But when Louise had gone downstairs to the refrigerator, I found I'd been wrong. Apparently Max Easter had nothing to say.

He stood up and said, "I think I'm going to try my wings, Mr. Hearn. Please don't help me. Louise would have insisted if she'd stayed, but I want to learn to find my way alone. I'm just going to cross the room to that other chair."

He was feeling his way across the carpet toward the other side of the room—almost exactly toward the place where the plaster had been chipped out of the wall to extract the bullet he had fired. He said, "Might as well learn to do this. For all I know—" He didn't finish the sentence, but we both knew what he'd started to say.

His hand touched the wall, then groped for the chair. He wasn't going to touch it from where he stood so I said, "To your right, about two steps."

"Thanks." He moved that way and his hand found the back of the straight chair against the wall. He turned and sat down in it, and I noticed that he sat hard, as one does when the surface one sits on is lower than one thought. As though a pillow might have been on the chair, but wasn't.

I'm not too bright, but I'm not too dumb. Pillow made me think of feathers. Blood, silk and feathers. A silk-covered chair pillow.

I had something, even if I didn't know what I had.

And just maybe, too, Max Easter's sense of direction, in walking for the chair, hadn't been as bad as it had seemed. He'd walked toward the place where the bullet had hit the wall. And if the chair were standing where he'd looked for it and if it had had a pillow on the seat the bullet would have gone through that pillow.

I didn't ask him if there'd been a silk pillow in that chair. I knew there had been.

I got a little scared.

Louise Easter was coming back up the stairs. Her heels clicked across the wood to the doorway and she came in with a tray that held three bottles and three glasses. She held the tray in front of me first and I took a glass and a bottle, but I wasn't thinking about beer.

I was thinking about blood. I knew now where the silk and feathers had come from.

I stood up and looked around me. I didn't see any blood, or anything that gave me an idea about blood, but I noticed something else unusual — the shade over the one window in the room. It was a double shade, very heavy, peculiarly constructed.

I got scareder. It must have shown in my voice when I asked about the shade.

Max answered it. He said, "Yes, I had that shade specially made, Mr. Hearn. I'm an amateur photographer, and use this room as my darkroom. Had the door fixed so it closes light-tight, too."

I counted back hours. It was almost three o'clock now; it must have been four to six hours since —

I said, "Max —" without realizing that I was calling him by his first name — "will you take off that bandage?"

I'd put down the bottle and glass without having poured myself a drink. When something's about to break I want my hands free.

Max Easter reached up uncertainly for the bandage around his head. Louise Easter said, "Max, don't! The doctor —" and then her eyes met mine and she knew there wasn't any use saying any more.

Max stood up and took the bandage off. He blinked and rubbed his eyes with uncertain hands. He said, "I can see! It blurs, but I'm beginning to—"

Then his eyes must have blurred a little less, because his look fixed on his wife's face.

And he did begin to see.

I made it as fast and as merciful—for Max Easter—as possible. I got her out of there, down to headquarters. And I took along the bottle that was labeled Boric Acid, but that contained the tetrianic acid that had been keeping him blind.

We brought Lloyd Eldred in. He wouldn't talk until two of the boys went out to his house with a search warrant. They found the suitcase buried in his back yard and brought it in with them. Then he talked.

Winding up something like that takes time. I didn't get home until almost eight. But I'd remembered to phone Marge to hold dinner.

I was still feeling shaky when I got there. But Marge thought talking it out would be good for me, so I talked. I told her about it:

"Lloyd Eldred and Louise Easter were planning to run away together. That was part of it. Another part of it is that Lloyd had embezzled some money from Springfield Chemical. He says about four thousand. He couldn't make it up; he'd lost it gambling. And they were due for an audit in two weeks—a routine annual audit—so he'd have had to lam anyway, even if it hadn't been for the Louise Easter part.

"But he wanted money to lam with, a stake to give them a start somewhere. He'd been putting through fake vouchers like mad and mailing checks to himself under other names. He had to have Max out of the way to do it; Max helped on the regular bookkeeping, besides his payroll work, and would have spotted it. And Wednesday of this week—day after tomorrow—is the semi-monthly payroll. And they pay the workmen, but not the white collar workers, in cash. With Max out of the way he could have got his hands on that money.

"So he rigged a little booby trap over the acid vat so that when Max pulled the pad of time slips, the jug would fall into the acid. That got rid of Max—but it wouldn't have kept him away long enough if Louise hadn't cooperated. And that was simple. He gave her some dilute tetrianic from the plant to substitute for the boric acid she cleaned his eyes with several times a day. She did it in a darkened room—I don't mean she pulled the shades down secretly, just that she told her husband it was supposed to be done that way. And she'd always do it a little before the doctor came each day so when he'd take the bandage off to check Max's eyes, they'd be about the same as they were the first time he'd examined them."

Marge looked at me wide-eyed. "Then he wasn't really blind, George! But I just said that because—"

"Whyever you said it," I told her, "you were right. But wait; I haven't got near the payoff yet. The murder wasn't something that was planned—it just came up. You see, Armin Robinson had learned that Lloyd Eldred and Louise Easter were having a clandestine affair. He probably saw them somewhere—anyway, he learned it somehow. Of course he didn't know about the embezzlement or that they were planning to run away together. But he knew Max's wife was cheating on him—and Max was his best friend. That was what he'd been worrying about, whether to tell Max or not.

"And he'd made up his mind to tell Max that evening, when he was alone with him. Louise must have guessed it—from his attitude or the way he talked to her when he came she guessed that he knew something and was going to tell Max after she'd gone.

"Then, just as she was leaving, Lloyd Eldred came. He'd dropped around to pay a duty call on Max, and had brought him a present, something he knew Max would like and that would help him keep amused while he was blind. Something that he could play with in bed."

Marge saw it coming. The back of her hand went to her mouth. "You mean—"

"Yes," I said. "A kitten. Max is crazy about cats. They'd had one and it had been killed by a car only a week before."

"George, what *color* was it?"

I said, "Louise met him at the front door and told him Max was talking to Armin and what she thought Armin was going to say. And Lloyd told her to run along, that he'd take care of things. He didn't tell her how.

"So she left and Lloyd went on into the house. He was much more worried about it than Louise had been. He realized that if that much of the truth came out, there'd be a showdown and probably his embezzlements at the plant would come out too, and that his whole plans would be shot and that he'd have to lam without the payroll money he was waiting for and counting on.

"He put the kitten in his pocket and went to where he knew Max kept a gun and got it. And he saw the cotton gloves and put them on. He went up the stairs on tiptoe and stood outside the door listening. And when he heard Armin Robinson say 'Max, there's something that I hate to—' he stepped into the room. And shot Armin as Armin saw him and stood up. It's a good thing Armin didn't speak his name, or he'd have shot Max too."

"But why did he toss the gun on the bed?"

"He didn't want to take it away with him. And his first thought was simply to confuse things by leaving the gun. And leaving the kitten—it just happened that he'd got it in a way that it couldn't be traced to him—and walking out. You see, it wasn't a planned murder. He was ad libbing as he went along.

"He walked nearer to the bed and tossed the gun onto it and then took the kitten out of his pocket and was holding it by the scruff of the neck to toss it after the gun. And then he saw that Max had got the gun first grab and was aiming it toward him, from only a couple of yards away. He dropped down to one knee to get under the shot if Max pulled the trigger. The muzzle of the gun went down as he dropped and Max shot. The bullet killed the cat—and buried itself in the wall after it'd gone through a silk pillow on the chair next to the wall.

"Then Max dropped the gun and it fell on the floor out of his reach—and the danger was over. Lloyd decided that his best bet was to make it look as nearly as possible like a burglary. He took the wallets and the watch and a suitcase from the closet. To make it look like a burglary, he can't leave the kitten—burglars don't leave kittens. On the way to the closet he'd dropped the dead kitten on the chair, on the pillow that the bullet went through, to have his hands free. When he got the suitcase, he put the kitten and the pillow into it together, because there was blood on the pillow.

"Meanwhile, Max hadn't moved—and he knew Max wouldn't dare to move until he heard the front door close. So he could take his time. He went through the downstairs and took silverware and a few other little things. And left. Period."

Marge said, "George, what color was that cat?"

"Marge," I said, "I don't believe in intuition or clairvoyance. Or in coincidence—not that much coincidence. So I'm damned if I'm going to tell you, ever."

But I guess that was enough of an answer for her—she didn't ask again.

THE FREAK SHOW
MURDERS

Carney Slang Used in The Freak Show Murders

Ball Game — Any concession in which the customer tries to win prizes by throwing balls to knock down milk bottles, dummies, et cetera.

Bally — (verb) To give a free show out front (on the bally platform) in order to draw a crowd. (noun) The free show described above.

Bally Cloth — The cloth that hangs from the edge of a platform down to the ground.

Banner — Picture on canvas hung in front of a freak show or other attraction, depicting the wonders to be seen inside.

Barker — The leather-lunged lad who persuades the crowd to buy tickets, and who introduces and describes the attractions on offer.

Blow-Down — The blowing down of a tent by a windstorm.

Blow-Off — (often merely "the blow") The show given in a partitioned-off end of a freak-show tent, and for which additional money is charged.

Canvasman — Employee whose principal job is to help put up and take down tents. He does other kinds of work while the carnival is operating.

Carney — A carnival, or anyone connected with a carnival.

Cooch — A type of dance, and if you don't know what a cooch dance is, better see one.

Doniker — The Chic Sale department. The group of outhouses put up somewhere on the lot.

Flash — The showy, but difficult-to-win, merchandise displayed as prizes at the concessions. Also an act is judged by how much flash it has, which means how spectacular it is.

G-Top — Gambling tent. Not open to outsiders; it's a small tent put up somewhere on the lots where the carneys can play cards or shoot dice among themselves.

Gaff — The hidden secret or gimmick of a trick. Not all acts, of course, have one. There's no gaff to a sword-swallower's act, for example.

Geek — A freak, usually a Negro, who eats glass, razor blades and almost anything else. Don't ask me how they can do it, but there's no gaff about it. A geek can chew up and swallow an old light bulb just as you'd eat an apple.

Gimmick — The same as "gaff" in one meaning. Also, another name for G-string.

Grind — The continuous spiel between ballys whereby the barker keeps customers coming in.

Half-and-Half — A half man, half woman.

Inside Money — Money obtained from customers inside the show through sale of souvenirs, usually, or tickets to the blow-off.

Jig Show — Dance show with colored performers. Negroes with a carney do not resent the term; it's accepted slang and not depreciatory as it would be in some sections of the country.

Nut — The overhead, the expenses. A show or concession is "on the nut" if not meeting expenses; "off the nut" if making money.

Mad Ball — A clairvoyant's crystal.

Mark — A customer or prospective customer, an outsider. "Sucker" used to be the common term; now "mark" is replacing it.

Mentalist — Fortuneteller or clairvoyant.

Midway — The open center area around which the tents are pitched and upon which they all front.

Mitt Camp — A fortuneteller's tent or booth. The term comes, of course, from palmistry, but is applied to any form of mentalism — phrenology, buddha papers, crystal-reading or what have you.

Penny Pitch — A concession in which customers pitch pennies at a board, winning prizes if pennies stop squarely within marked-off areas.

Pincushion — The "Human Pincushion" of the freak show; a man who sticks pins and needles into his skin for the edification of the public.

Pitch — To sell something to a group of marks.

Props — The physical properties of a show.

Side Wall — The straight canvas side of a tent, usually not fastened down at the bottom.

Sloughed — Not permitted to operate. If the law closes a show or concession, it is sloughed.

Slum — Cheap concession prizes; distinguished from flash, the showy but hard-to-get prizes.

Spiel — To talk.

Sucker — Same as "mark."

Teardown — The dismantling of the show and taking down of the tents to travel to the next town.

Tip — A group of marks. A barker "turns a tip" when he gets a good percentage of them to buy tickets for the show.

Top — A tent.

Chapter I: "Step Right Up, Folks!"

Trouble and murder were just about the farthest things from my mind, right then. I was spieling, but my mouth did that for me without my mind having to tell it what to do, and while I talked I was staring out up the midway and thinking how swell it was to be back with the carney again.

It felt good to be standing on a platform with a tip of marks out there looking up with their yaps open while I told them what we had for them inside the top.

"Step right up close, folks!" I told them. "That's it, right up to the edge of the platform. We're going to put on a free show, a big free show, right out here on the platform, and it isn't going to cost you one penny to see it. Not one single, solitary penny—"

And back over my shoulder I yelled, "Colonel bally. Bugs bally."

I hit the bass drum a few thumping boomps while I waited for them to come out from the top. It was going to be a fair-sized tip, for the first one of the afternoon. Usual percentage of kids and suckers.

I gave them the old Pete Gaynor smile and boomped the drum again. Some marks who'd been gawking at the girl-show front turned around and came over.

"Right now, friends, right now, I'm going to call out on this platform a few of the strange people of the Wonderworld top! The most amazing and astounding people you have ever seen. Right out here on the platform to meet you! Here comes one now—"

There's nothing much to barking for a freak show if you've got the gift of gab. It doesn't matter much what you say, just so you keep saying it impressively. You don't even have to yell any more, because the loud-speaker system does that for you. Brass-lunged barkers are one with Ninevah and Tyre.

"Yes, folks, here he is! The famous *Colonel Toots!* The smallest and one of the most brilliant men alive in the world today! Meet Colonel Toots, just thirty-four inches tall from his heels to the top of his head. A midget among midgets, folks, and a talented and versatile entertainer to boot. Inside the tent, Colonel Toots will show you, I can promise each and every one of you, the most amazing—"

I hadn't been looking at them because I'd turned to face Colonel Toots as he came on. But something in the way the Colonel was looking at the tip made me turn around to see what was wrong with them.

What was wrong was that they weren't looking at Colonel Toots nor at me; they were gawking past us, over and around the platform. And I heard voices and excitement back there, now that my attention followed the direction of their gaze.

The ticket man at my right was turning around, too. His head was lower than mine and he could see under the banners into the entrance. I saw him nod that way and start to get out of the ticket box.

He said to me, "Hold it, Pete. No bally."

"Huh? You mean I should let the—"

"Yeah, let the tip go. Won't be opening yet."

He shoved the roll of tickets under his arm and started back at a half run.

I said into the microphone, "Folks, sorry, but we're not quite ready to open yet. Come back in a little while—and we'll show you the best show—"

I realized my tongue was getting loose again and I was darned curious to see what was wrong inside the top. So I cut it short and switched off the mike. Colonel Toots was already gone off the platform.

Bugs, I thought—something's happened to Bugs Cartier. I'd called him for the bally and he hadn't shown up. Of course you never can count on a pincushion; they're a bit off or they wouldn't go around sticking pins in themselves to keep from having to work.

In under the top there was a knot of people gathered around Bugs' platform. It looked like a bigger crowd than it was, because one of them was Bessie Williams, our fat woman. I tried to look over Bessie's shoulder, but Bessie's shoulders aren't made to be looked over, unless you don't want to look in a downward direction.

I could see that the platform was empty, that the bally cloth had been thrown up over the edge and that they were staring at something on the grass under the platform. But Bessie wasn't transparent and I couldn't tell what it was.

Before I could ask any questions there was a hand on my shoulder, shoving me aside. I turned angrily and then curbed the vitriol I was set to hand whoever it was. Because it was Red Lewis, the Haverton copper, who'd drawn the day shift of patrolling the carney grounds. And Red Lewis was six feet four and built along the lines of a more famous Louis. Besides, he had red hair and a pugnacious disposition; not a guy to be cussed out casually without risking a fight.

So I stepped aside, waiting for what was going to happen when he tried to push Bessie. That was going to be worth watching.

But even a copper, it proved, had more sense than to try that. He went around her, shoving his way in between Bessie and Stella Alleman, and I followed his interference and got through.

It was Al Hryner who was under the platform.

He was dead; there wasn't any doubt about that because the back of his head was bashed in. And lying there beside him was a tent stake with dark stains on the end of it.

Red Lewis was glowering at us when he turned. He said, "All right, who done it?"

Stella Alleman, the snake girl, laughed with a sound that was near hysteria. I was behind her, to one side, and I put my hands on her shoulders and said, "Watch it, kid. Don't go haywire."

Somebody, I think it was Bugs, started in to tell the copper what had happened, but I didn't listen. I could feel Stella's shoulders trembling under my hands, and I pulled her back from the crowd, turning her around to face me so her back would be toward the excitement.

"Take it easy, honey," I said, "your mascara is smearing something awful. Don't let a little thing like a murder get you down."

"But why would anyone have —"

"Probably somebody found out Al's dice were crooked, honey. Let's get out of here. I'll buy you a coke."

I took her arm and, before she could object, started to take her out the entrance to the midway. Then I remembered there was a crowd out there and lifted the side wall instead.

"We'll cut through a couple of the tops," I suggested.

But as we cut under the next side wall I rather wished we hadn't. The top next to the freak show is the waxworks — the Chamber of Horrors — and it's not the place to take a girl to make her forget a murder. The place is full of killers and their kills, and some of them are pretty convincing stuff, for wax.

So I hurried Stella toward the entrance, trying to talk fast. "We'll cut out here," I said. "Come on, honey."

But she pulled loose, and when I turned around she was powdering her nose. She said, "I must look awful, Pete. I can't go outside looking —"

So it was all right, and she was over it and not going to take a tailspin. I grinned in relief. There wasn't any hurry now.

"What gave, back there?" I asked her. "Who found him, and what's it all about?"

"Bugs found him," she said. "He — let's see, how did it happen? Oh, yes; you yelled back for Bugs and the colonel to come out for the bally, and Bugs couldn't find his pins — those hatpins, you know. He hunted around and then thought maybe they'd gone between the boards of his platform and were under it. He lifted up the cloth and — well, he saw Al there."

I nodded. Way in the distance somewhere I heard the wail of a siren that meant the rest of the coppers were coming. I realized, suddenly, that Red wouldn't have had time to send for them. I asked Stella, "Who turned it in?"

"Lee Werner, I guess. He went out the side wall and I guess he ran over to the phone in the front wagon."

We went out into the midway by the front entrance of the waxworks. I saw Lee hurrying back toward the freak show. I don't like Lee much, but I felt sorry for him right now. He was the guy who'd be out money on account of this. A Saturday afternoon, too.

He moved past us without noticing, but I said, "Hey, Lee," and he turned. I said, "Tough break. How long'll we be sloughed?"

He ran his handkerchief across his forehead. "God knows, Pete. Maybe later in the afternoon—Stick on the lot. Lord, this kind of weather—"

He looked up at the clear-blue sky and I knew what he was thinking. All week it had rained, off and on. All week had been on the nut, strictly loss, and now came Saturday, the big day of the week and perfect weather. Then somebody has to kill a canvasman. I really felt sorry for Lee. And you can only guess what the law's going to do in a case like that.

Stella and I strolled across to the dog wagon and got a couple of cokes.

I said, "Still prefer the snakes to me?"

"Pete, can't you . . . can't you—"

"Forget? Nope. Can't. I stayed away from the carney three months and missed the best part of the season. I tried four different jobs and three different cities. No go. Here I am back."

"You're carney, Pete. You'd never be happy away from it. But there are other carnivals. Why didn't you get with Royal American or Dodson or somebody else?"

"Nuts to them," I said. "It wasn't the carney. It was you — and those damn snakes. I'm jealous of them. Everything reminds me of them. A thousand miles away I see spaghetti and I think of Black King coiling around you, and wish it was me."

"But you couldn't —"

"I could try, dammit. Say, this Al Hryner — there wasn't any *reason*, was there, for your nearly getting hysterical, was there? I mean, uh, you hadn't fallen for him, or anything, had you?"

She shook her head. "I . . . I almost hated the guy, Pete. Since he's dead now and you can't go starting a fight over it, I might as well admit he's been making passes. But —"

"When did he join the carney?"

"Just two weeks ago."

"Funny," I said. "Alive, the guy was just another canvasman. Dead, he stops the show. Say, let's take a turn on the Ferris wheel. I haven't ridden a Ferris wheel since I was a kid."

She looked at me blankly. "Huh? *Us*, ride a Ferris wheel?"

"Why not? Let's be suckers. Let's ride the merry-go-round and take in the dippyhouse and the jig show. Let's gawk at the geek. The only people who never see a carney are the carneys."

"You're on. Let's." I had her smiling now.

So we gave the merry-gcc a whirl, took in Little Harlem and had Stella's palm read at the mitt camp. She wouldn't tell me what they told her there. Then we tried the Ferris wheel.

It was funny, to be up on top of the world like we were when our car was way up there. Looking down on the midway full of toy tents and toy people walking around and knowing that you were seeing the mixing of two worlds down there. The carneys and the outsiders.

And there was an ugly side of each. Lies and gaffs and deceit and never give a sucker an even break, on the carney's part. But the marks, too. It was because the marks were what they were that the carneys had to be that way. It was larceny in their hearts that made them mob the gambling concessions, trying to get something for nothing; lust that led them into the girl shows; morbid curiosity that made them like to see a man stick pins into his skin or a fire-eater put a blow torch in his mouth.

It was the subconscious desire to see a man die that made them stand open-mouthed every evening to watch Vince Piranelli ride a bicycle down that steep, narrow track, loop it in the air, and land in the net. A small net; that was why they watched. He might miss.

It was the ugliness that sent them into the waxworks to see the horrible and gory reproductions of famous crimes and criminals. There was red in that set-up, and they paid to see the red of blood, Bluebeard and Jack the Ripper, and Burke and Hare — they paid their fifteen cents and came. Offer a waxworks of, say, Galileo working on a telescope, young Abe Lincoln doing sums on the back of a shovel, things like that, and what people would pay fifteen cents to get in? A few. But you'd starve.

Then the Ferris wheel went round again and this time, up on top, I forgot all that and saw it as it should be seen. The beauty and pageantry, and brave bright pennants waving in the wind, the brave bright brass of the carney band and the red of their uniforms. The ripple of canvas and the ripple of laughter and the ripple of movement.

Beside me, Stella said, "Gee, Pete. Why didn't we ever think of doing this before? It's . . . it's swell."

I grinned at her. "Let's get married and buy a Ferris wheel, honey. We'll live in it and keep it running all the time. With walls around the cars and each a separate room but some with windows, so we can watch the world go round."

"And a room for Black King? Can I keep Black King?"

"Sure. But to even it up, we ought to have some pet mongeese, too. I mean, mongooses. Or do I?"

"One mongoose," said Stella firmly. "Then you won't have to worry."

"Unless it has mongoslings. Then they'll grow up and what'll they be?"

"Hey," said a voice, and I looked around and our car was stopped at the exit runway. Red Lewis was yelling at me. "You, Pete."

I got out of the car reluctantly and helped Stella down. We walked over to the copper.

"Opening already?" I asked him.

"No. Lieutenant Helsing wants you. He's in charge over there."

I turned back to Stella. "It's the inquisition," I told her. "Look, you go up to the chow-top and have some coffee and I'll be there as soon as I'm through with the —"

"Better not make a date like that," Red cut in.

And when I turned to stare at him blankly, he added, "I think the looie's going to take you in — for murder."

He wasn't smiling, either.

Chapter II: "You Killed Him!"

There was still a crowd around the freak-show front, although the bally platform was empty and the side wall dropped down, so there wasn't a thing for them to see. But the crowd was bigger than I'd ever seen it. A swell tip, and I could have turned all of them, too, if I could have climbed the platform to spiel. Wouldn't even have needed a bally show.

Except myself.

"Folks, right out here on this platform the one and only Pete Gaynor, living proof of the stupidity of John Law. He's just been told he's going to be pinched for killing a mug he met the night before and never said anything more important to than 'You're faded.' Yes sir, folks, Pete Gaynor, the original and only —"

Yes, it would have been a howl.

Red pushed us through the crowd and past the two coppers who were guarding the entrance, and we went in under the side wall.

I couldn't see any coppers around except one who was standing back against the end platform, the one Bessie sits on. The carneys were gathered around in little groups, talking. None of the groups were around Bugs Cartier's platform. Its bally cloth was folded back, so I could see under it, but someone had put a cloth over the thing that lay there. Somehow, it seemed symbolic of carnival that the cloth was crimson velvet with gold fringe.

Red Lewis was looking about, obviously puzzled. He said, "Wonder where the looie went, him and the others?"

"Maybe the doniker," I said, "but a better guess is they're holding court in the blow-off."

Red glowered at me. "Whyn't you guys talk English?" he wanted to know.

I grinned, because it hadn't occurred to me I was talking anything else. You forget, sometimes.

I said, "The blow-off, my carrot-topped comrade, is where we hold the cooch-blow for the inside money, except that this week in Haverton it got sloughed. Now don't get excited. It's that partitioned-off section of the tent down at the other end. My guess is they'd have decided it was a good private place to interview people."

My guess was right, and Lieutenant Helsing—or, anyway, a heavy-set man with a dull, beefy face whom I took to be the lieutenant—was sitting on the edge of the cooch stage with his round-toed black brogans dangling over the footlights. He looked ridiculously out of place there. Between him and Mae Cole, our cooch gal, being on that stage, I'd take Mae even on a rainy Monday. There were two other coppers standing around, one of them with an open notebook and a well-chewed pencil.

Red Lewis said, "Here's Gaynor, lieutenant," and shoved me forward.

Helsing looked at me expressionlessly and asked, "Why'd you kill this Al Hryner?"

I wanted to laugh, but I didn't. I said, "I'll bet you ask that of all the boys. I hardly even knew Al Hryner. I met him last night."

"Where?"

"In the G-top, in a crap game."

"The G-top? You mean the gambling tent?"

I nodded. "Yeah," I said, "and I lost money. Nine bucks. But I don't kill people for nine bucks; it's under union scale. Ten bucks for beating somebody up, fifteen for mayhem, and for murder it's twenty-five."

He slid down off the stage and leaned against it instead. "A smart guy, eh?"

I thought it over. Maybe I wasn't being smart.

"Look," I said, "we're getting off on the wrong foot. Seriously, I saw Al Hryner for the first time in my life yesterday evening. He joined the carney while I was away. Two weeks ago, I understand. I came back yesterday. I didn't kill him and I haven't the faintest idea who did."

"What time'd you see him last?"

"It would have been around two o'clock. We ran until a little after twelve thirty. I hit the G-top about one, and was in the game maybe an hour. Hryner was still there when I left. I turned in. My bunk's in the third of those four cars on the siding."

Helsing took a long cigar out of his pocket and stuck it in his face. He said, "When'd you find out Hryner had been using crooked dice to take you with?"

"I didn't know. Was he?"

"You knew, Gaynor. We got a statement on that."

For a minute it left me blank. Then I began to see why the coppers were throwing the book at me. Somebody'd heard my casual remark to Stella, "Probably someone found Al's dice were crooked."

And whoever it was, was deliberately trying to get me in trouble when they reported it. Because from my tone of voice they'd have known I was making a casual guess and not an accusation.

"Were Al's dice crooked?" I asked.

Helsing jerked his thumb toward two envelopes that were lying on the edge of the footlights behind him. He said, "Pair in each side pocket. We'll saw 'em to make sure, but I rolled each pair a dozen times and one of 'em gave eight sevens out of twelve rolls."

"Red, transparent dice?"

The lieutenant nodded.

"Those are the ones used in the game last night then," I told him, "but I didn't even know they were Hryner's. The game was going when I wandered into the G-top and I left before they quit."

"Who was still playing when you left?"

I thought a minute. "Besides Al Hryner, just two. Bugs Cartier — the pincushion — and Gus."

"Who's Gus?"

"Gus Smith. Owns and runs the waxworks."

"How much did he and — uh — this Cartier drop?"

I shrugged. "You'll have to ask them. I wasn't keeping books."

"Heavy game?"

"No. Bugs was shooting dimes; he couldn't have lost much. Gus was in the two-bit class. I lost as much as nine bucks because I ran into a bad streak on doubling up when I had the dice myself. Couldn't have been the dice, either."

"Why not?"

"Snake-eyes, threes, and box cars. Dice could be loaded to crap one way or another, but not all three. I must have had the straight pair, because after five craps I got Little Joe for a point, and had nine or ten rolls for it before I sevened out."

Everything was going O.K., I thought. I'd started out wrong, but by now it was going O.K. Only I was in a hurry to get back to Stella, and, anyway, I didn't know any more to tell the coppers.

I said, "How much longer before we can open up?"

"Maybe an hour. But you won't be doing the barking, Gaynor. We're taking you along; the chief wants to talk to you."

"Huh?" I said, and began to lose my temper again, just a little. "You're crazy. Why pick on *me?* Dammit, even if I *had* known the dice were crooked, I wouldn't have done —"

"That isn't why you killed him. Don't play dumb, Gaynor. We got the inside dope and you're the *only* guy around here with a motive. Why'd you leave the carnival three months ago?"

"Personal reasons. And they couldn't have anything to do with Al Hryner because he wasn't around then."

"Sure, they didn't. We know what they were. You left because you were soft on this broad who handles the snakes and she wouldn't give you a tumble and then —"

I felt it coming, and I tried to stop him; I didn't *want* to hit a copper and get myself in a jam. I tried to interrupt. I said, "Shut up, goddam —" But he cut in and kept on.

"— and then you learned somewhere that this Al was making —"

My fist against his jaw bent him back over the footlights of the cooch stage, and then I was grabbed from behind and whirled around. And Red Lewis was wading in before I could get set for him. I saw his fist coming at my face, but I was off balance and couldn't duck. It was a fist the size of a small ham and it had Red's two-twenty pounds back of it. It hit, and the lights went out.

It was two o'clock when Lee Werner, my boss, got in to see me at the Haverton hoosegow. Two in the morning, I mean.

He spent the first couple of minutes cussing, and didn't repeat himself once. Then he said, "Come on, I put up bail for you. God knows why."

"Bail? On a murder charge?"

"You dimwit, there isn't any murder charge against you. You're in for slugging a cop — and why'd you have to pick a looie?"

"I'd slug him again, Lee, if he —"

"Listen, you're going to behave yourself or I'll pull that bail and let you sit here and rot. We pull town tomorrow night, and I'm trying to get this thing squared before then. Lord, I've seen the mayor of this burg and the chief of police, and— Hell, if they wanted to, they could hold *all* of us here until they got that murder settled."

I whistled. "You mean they could hold the whole carney—a couple or three hundred people, just because a canvasman gets killed?"

"Not the whole carney, no. But the material witnesses, and that'd put an awful dent in my show. Lucky our next hop is a short one; I had to promise I'd let 'em be back for the inquest. That's one day we're going to lose as it is."

"And for slugging the looie, how about that? Will I have to come back another day to stand trial for that?"

"We're trying to get the charge killed. Listen, Helsing isn't such a bad guy. I put Stella to work on him, and—"

"You what?"

"Sure. And he's beginning to see the light. He realizes, after he talked with her awhile, that he popped off the wrong side of his mouth. He's apologized to her for it. They're across the street waiting for us."

"They? You mean Helsing and Stella?"

"Yeah. I insisted on being the one to come and get you. I knew if you saw Helsing again before I explained, you'd pop off and then it'd be too late—he couldn't withdraw that charge and save his face. And his face ain't so hot now. You did it no good."

I grinned. "Neither is my jaw. But it was the grounds copper, Red, who did that. All right, what we waiting for?"

"You're sure you'll—"

"Positively. If he's apologized to Stella, it's O.K. by me."

"Come on, then."

My release was already arranged and the turnkey let us out.

I was broke at the moment, so I borrowed a buck from Lee Werner and gave it to the turnkey. He'd given me a pack of cigarettes early in the evening and there are times when a pack of fags are worth a buck.

Helsing stood up warily when Lee and I walked into the quiet little bar which was right across the street from the station.

I said "hello" to Stella first and then, to Helsing, "Lieutenant, I understand you've taken back what caused it, so I'm sorry I lost my temper this afternoon. Shake on it?"

I put out my hand and he took it and grinned.

"My fault," he said, "but I didn't know Miss Alleman then. Have a drink?"

"The round's on me," I said as we sat down. "My coming-out party. Only Lee'll pay for it and put it on the books. Yes, lieutenant, Stella's a swell gal and don't let the snakes fool you. She was abandoned as a waif and a python adopted her and brought her up, so it isn't her fault."

"Not quite that, lieutenant," said Stella. "My folks were carney and I was brought up in a side show. I liked to play with snakes, almost in my crib, and never acquired the dislike of them that most people have."

"The ones you use have had their fangs pulled?"

Stella shook her head. "They're bull snakes and haven't any fangs to pull. They're quite friendly—anybody can handle them."

"Not me," said Helsing, firmly.

"Anybody can handle them," I said, "but few of us could be as decorative in doing it as Stella is."

After our drinks came, Lee cleared his throat. He said, "Uh—about those charges against Pete, lieutenant—are you—uh—going to press them?"

Helsing looked at me, and for once I decided to keep my mouth shut and let Lee and Stella handle him. They'd been doing all right, so far.

"Just one thing," Helsing said, "before I decide to withdraw them. You got no hard feelings against Lewis, have you, Gaynor?"

I shook my head. "Not a thing. What he did was in line of duty; I swung first."

So that's how it was I was back at the loud-speaker by Sunday and helping with tear-down Sunday night, and making the forty-mile hop to Wilmot. I learned later that Lee had got opened by six o'clock and caught the evening crowd, but that the lost afternoon had cost him plenty.

We put up the top in Wilmot Monday in a drizzling rain that looked as though it would last all week. Lee wandered about disconsolately, without even a hat on, and the rain running down the back of his neck. I felt very sorry for the guy.

Chapter III: Black King

Monday afternoon the rain was harder, and the Wilmot cops came. The chief of police himself, and he was plenty hard-boiled. No cooch-blow, no mitt camp, and if we'd had a half-and-half, that would have been sloughed, too. He seemed a little sorry we didn't have one. The police chief's name was Seton, William L. Seton.

It was going to be a bad week; there wasn't any doubt about that. Rain or no rain.

Seton went up and down the midway, asking questions about the set-up on each of the concessions, and he sloughed three of them that were too near to gambling to suit him. He wanted to see the costumes the girls in the girl show wore, or would wear if it ever stopped raining.

Yes, it was going to be a great week in Wilmot. And already some of the wagons were sinking in to the hubs. Shavings fought mud, and the shavings couldn't win.

But Seton said he wasn't going to worry himself about our little murder. It had happened at Haverton, and the Haverton cops could have it. The inquest was for Wednesday morning, he told us, and we'd all better go over there. All of us from the freak show, that is, and any of the others who knew Al Hryner, canvasman, deceased.

Lee Werner did the only thing possible. He introduced Seton to Mae Cole, our cooch girl, and then went away and left 'em, after giving Mae the office. If the chief was susceptible, Mae might talk him into letting her operate. If she did, Lee might make enough profit to wash out last week's losses, because the blow-off was our gravy.

Monday evening it was still drizzling. Only a few kids waded out to see the carney, and none of the shows opened.

The only bright spot was that nobody could find Mae Cole around the lot, and Lee began to hope for the best. Or the worst, depending strictly upon one's point of view.

At nine it was still raining. Not a chance of giving a single show. We got a rummy game going in the G-top and played for nickels until a little after midnight.

Using a flashlight, I picked my way around back of the tents toward the sleepers. I was behind the freak-show top when I remembered the magazine I'd bought that afternoon and had left on Stella's platform. Maybe I'd read a story before I went to sleep.

I ducked in under the side wall, found myself behind Bessie's platform, and went around it. I played the flashlight ahead of me toward Stella's platform and then said, "What the hell?"

Because the snake box was open! Stella kept her snakes in a red tin trunk, specially made with inset screen gratings in the ends. Now the lid of it was wide open, leaning back against the curtain post behind it.

I blinked my eyes and looked again to make sure it wasn't an optical illusion. Stella certainly wouldn't have left it open, and nobody else would have had reason for opening it, unless—unless they wanted to steal snakes. Snakes — good ones — cost money all right. But they're difficult things to peddle to a fence in his right mind.

Just the same I took the rest of the distance to the platform on the double-quick to get that lid down again. I don't know why I thought there was any hurry — unless that lid had just been opened, which was improbable — the snakes would be gone if they were going.

I jumped up on the platform and looked down into the box. Two of the bulls were still in there, the two smaller ones. Black King was gone.

I put the lid down, and I must have slammed it because somebody said, "What's all the noise, dammit?" and I turned the beam of my flash toward the sound of Bugs Cartier's voice.

He was sitting up on his own platform, wrapped in a blanket and blinking sleepily at me.

I said, "It's me, Pete Gaynor. Somebody swiped Black King."

"Huh?"

I jumped down off the platform, my first intention being to go to Lee's trailer and tell him about it. But as my feet hit the soft turf it occurred to me that maybe Black King had escaped because, after all, the lid had been open accidentally. And if so, he might still be near at hand.

It wouldn't hurt to take a look, at least around and under the platform. I started around back of it, the flashlight held out ahead of me and aimed down at the grass.

But I didn't get there because something heavy smacked down on my wrist and knocked the flashlight out of my hand. I jumped back with an involuntary yowl, thinking my wrist was broken.

The flashlight hit the grass, still burning, but it had twisted in its fall and shone backward on me. Then something hit it a wallop and the freak-show top was in utter darkness.

I kept on backing away, my feet making no sound on the turf

by which I could be followed, and I was glad of that. I'm as brave as the next guy, maybe, but with what might be a broken wrist I had no inclination to tangle with a man armed with a tent stake in utter darkness.

But he didn't come after me. I heard the rustle of canvas as though the side wall behind the platform was being lifted and dropped again.

Bugs' voice, still sleepy, said, "What the *hell* are you doing? And what about Black—"

I said, "Got a flashlight, Bugs? Turn it on!" And then I moved again, quick, because the guy with the tent stake might have been bluffing with the side-wall canvas, and I didn't want to locate myself for him by talking and then staying put.

Bugs said, "Sure. Uh—" And then a beam of light flashed out from his platform, bracketed me, and then went to Stella's platform.

Bugs was throwing off his blanket and he jumped down and came toward me. He had the flashlight in one hand and a long, sharp-looking stiletto in the other. He said, "You hurt, Pete? Where's the guy?"

I told him quickly what had happened, and Bugs said, "Wait a minute," and did what I hadn't thought of doing; ran across to the center pole and plugged in the top lights.

Then, together, we made the circuit of Stella's platform and the ones near it, and even looked underneath the bally cloths. The guy was gone. What made me sure was that just outside the side wall, at about the point where I thought I'd heard it rustle, we found a tent stake lying.

There were what might be called tracks, too, but they were utterly shapeless in the soggy grass, and after a few paces they petered out completely in the well-tracked area around behind the tops.

"Guy's gone," said Bugs. "Say, how's your wrist? How's about getting a doc?"

I'd been wriggling my fingers experimentally and they worked. I said, "I'm pretty sure nothing's busted. Just a bruise. Look, you go wake up Lee Werner. I'm going back to the top. In case —"

I found I didn't know what I meant by "in case" so I went back under the side wall before I had to finish it.

I took a look around for Black King but couldn't find a sign of him. If he was really gone it was going to be another wallop in the pocketbook for Lee Werner; it was he, not Stella, who owned the snakes. Black King had cost plenty shekels, too.

Not a sign of him. I went out the midway entrance and looked under the platform. When I straightened up I saw a man standing just the other side of it.

He said, "Gaynor?"

"Helsing," I said, "how'd you get over here?"

"Just got off duty and drove over. It's only forty miles. Not much doing, huh?"

"Depends on how you look at it," I told him. I was wondering whether I'd better tell him what happened just now. It might mean another investigation that would cost Lee a lot more than the loss of a seven-foot worm.

Helsing said, "I thought this'd be the shank of the evening for you carneys. It's only a few minutes after twelve. Where is everybody?"

Lee Werner's voice from inside the top yelled out, "Hey, Pete! Where are you?"

So Helsing was going to find out anyway, and maybe it would be all for the best. So I said, "It isn't as quiet as it looks, lieutenant. Come on in."

And that way I got a chance to explain to him and to Lee at the same time. Lee surprised me by taking it quietly and calmly.

He insisted on taking me over to Gus Smith first. Gus wasn't a doctor, but he'd picked up a bit of medical knowledge — maybe from studying anatomy while he was learning to make wax figures. Anyway, when Gus felt my wrist carefully and said it wasn't broken, Lee believed him. I was already convinced.

Then we routed out all the men who worked for Lee — except Slim Norris, the ticket man, who'd gone in to town and wasn't back yet — and made a systematic search of the top and the area around it. The rest of the carney lot would have to wait till daylight for a systematic search, although we covered it with flashlights and lanterns as well as we could. No sign of Black King.

Helsing stuck by me; maybe because he liked me — or maybe to see I didn't swipe any more snakes.

He said, "How's about the police — I mean, the Wilmot police. You got to call them."

I ducked the issue. "That's up to Lee," I said. "It's his worm got swiped — if it *was* swiped and didn't just escape. It's up to him to make a complaint."

Helsing snorted. "Don't be a dope. You were attacked. The guy who slapped you on the wrist with a tent stake would just as soon have parted your hair with it."

He paused a minute and then added quietly, "Like he parted Al Hryner's hair with it. Remember what the back of Hryner's head looked like."

Neither of us said anything for a minute and then he said, "Well?"

"Well, what?"

Helsing spat disgustedly into a puddle momentarily illuminated by the beam of his flashlight. He said, "You damn carneys. You don't like coppers, do you?"

"Do you know Chief Seton, here in Wilmot?"

"All right, so, off the record, he's a louse. He's still better than having your head bashed in."

"That's a matter of taste," I told him. "Shall we take a look through the waxworks?"

We ducked under the side wall of the waxworks tent and I found the plug that switched the lights on. Then we went around the aisle, taking one exhibit at a time, and looking carefully, using our flashlights wherever there was a dark shadow.

"This stuff is good," Helsing said. He was looking at a lifesize wax figure of Pierre Garroux driving his shiv into the back of a man seated at a table. "Only this guy's holding his knife wrong."

"Apache style," I said. "Yeah, this stuff is good. And you won't find Gus pulling any boners like a shiv held wrong. He's maybe the best waxworks man in the country. Only there isn't any money in waxworks since the gay Nineties, and that puts him with Tookerman Shows. He's a bug on authenticity."

"Hey, look—nuts, I thought that was a snake."

We moved down in front of the exhibit Helsing was looking at. It was a cheerful scene in which a murderer was getting ready to hang the victim he had already throttled with his hands. A coil of rope had fooled Helsing.

"Danny Watson," I said. "Killed six people for insurance before they got him, for the murder you see being enacted before your very eyes. It was intended to be taken for a suicide by hanging, but he very stupidly forgot the chair his victim was supposed to have stepped off from."

Helsing looked at me curiously. "Friend of yours?"

I grinned. "Nope, I used to spiel for Gus part of the time last season. Come on, meet the rest of his menagerie.

"Here's Tommy Benno, the bank bandit, in the very act of backing away from the scene of his crime—one of his earlier crimes—with a blazing Tommy-gun in his hands. And, by the way, lieutenant, what ever happened to Tommy? Is he still kicking around loose or did they catch him and burn him?"

"Nobody's heard of him since that Eltinge bank job six months ago," said Helsing. "Half a million bucks, so I guess he's retired all right. That's a darn good likeness of him."

"They're all good likenesses," I said. "Take that next one, Butch Davis. Gus traveled a hundred miles and back just to study Butch in court while he was being tried. Had good photos and descriptions to work from, too, but he still went that far just to look at the guy. That was ten years ago; I read recently Davis was applying for a pardon. Did he get it?"

Helsing shrugged. "Before my time, I guess. I never heard of Butch Davis. No, don't tell me. Let's look for that damn snake instead."

We looked thoroughly. It was no dice as far as the waxworks tent was concerned.

As we went out under the side wall, Helsing brought it up again about the Wilmot police. I listened patiently, and then interrupted.

"Look," I said, "as far as I'm concerned, *you're* the police. You know about it and that lets me out."

"You damn fool, don't you realize that this is part of the same business as the Hryner murder? That this isn't just somebody slapping you on the wrist and swiping a snake?"

"All the more reason why it's your baby. The Wilmot police said they wouldn't horn in on the murder. They horned in on everything else from the size of the gimmicks in the jig show to the size of the squares on the penny-pitch boards."

I took him back to see Lee Werner, and Lee looked at it the same way I did. As far as he was concerned, the snake had merely escaped and would be found in the morning. And it was nobody's loss but his; Black King was as harmless as a kitten and wouldn't hurt anybody if he had gone off the lot.

Helsing said, "But dammit —"

Lee ran his fingers through what hair he had left, as though he was going to tear it out by the roots. He said, with pleading in his voice, "Listen, suppose word gets around there's a loose snake around the carney. How many people are going to come if that gets in the Wilmot papers? And will they publish that the snake is nonpoisonous and tame? They will not; they'll make a scare story out of it. And since two weeks ago we're on the nut; we *need* a good play here — or else. Have a heart, lieutenant."

Helsing thought a minute and then shrugged. He said, "Got a phone wire out here?"

"Sure, over in the pay wagon. Want to use it?"

"I'll phone the chief at Haverton. Maybe he'll say it's O.K. for me to stay over here until the inquest. Can you put me up?"

"Put you up?" Lee grinned for the first time in an hour. "Hell, you can have my trailer. I'll bunk with the boys."

Helsing said, "Lead me to the phone. If it's O.K. by my boss —"

And it was.

Chapter IV: Pincushion

Tuesday morning and, for a change, it rained.

I heard it on the roof of the bunk car and I turned over and tried to go back to sleep. But the patter of rain on a roof isn't a soothing sound to a carney. If sounds can have opposites, the patter of rain on roof or canvas is the opposite of the patter of silver on a ticket ledge.

So I got up and dressed. Anyway, I wanted to see Stella and to find out if Black King was back. An idea had occurred to me; just maybe, if Black King had escaped and not been stolen, he would have found Stella. Maybe he'd have hunted her out, and had been curled under her bunk while we had looked for him. I don't know whether snakes are that intelligent or not.

But Black King was still gone. Stella was disconsolate; I found her out in the rain, hunting Black King. I helped awhile, and then insisted on taking her into the chow top for coffee. I tried to talk her into a cheerful frame of mind, but I was kind of in the dumps myself, and I suppose my cheerfulness sounded forced.

Back in the freak-show top, we found Lee Warner talking to himself. He'd had a quarrel with Ralph Chapman, our prestidigitator, and Ralph had almost quit on him. That would have been bad; with the cooch and the mitt camp out, Ralph was getting the only inside money in the show. At the end of his sleight-of-hand routine, Ralph pitched an envelope of tricks that pulled in quite a few quarters.

"Only two weeks from the end of the season," Lee was moaning, "and all we need is a blow-down."

I left Stella with Lee and went over to talk to Ralph Chapman.

I said, "Listen, Ralph, give the boss a break. The guy's half screwy. He's been taking—"

"Sure, Pete, but so have the rest of us. Dammit, I'm on percentage, and *I* haven't been getting rich, either. So why does he got to take it out on me, by calling me—"

"With you," I told him, "whatever he called you is practically a compliment. Now listen, Ralph—" And I went on and got him so mad at me, I knew he'd forget about Lee.

Then I went back to Lee and Stella.

"Where's Helsing?" I asked Lee.

"Drove over to Haverton. Wanted to get his toothbrush or something. He'll be back and stay here tonight again. Then tomorrow, the blasted inquest. Listen, if the weather's good tomorrow—"

"If it is, we'll go early," I told him, "and we'll talk them into getting our testimony quick—or if it's going to drag on, maybe we can get a postponement at noon and get back here in time to work."

Lee said, "It'll probably rain. It looks like an all-week rain to me. All we need is a storm and a blow-down."

"All we need is to keep our heads," I told him. "It can't rain forever. And go easy on Ralph. He's strictly prima donna and you know it."

"What's eating him is that Mae Cole isn't back. He's been making a play for Mae, and he blames me for sicking her on Seton. Hell, Mae can't see Chapman with a telescope."

I whistled. "Mae isn't back? What you suppose happened?"

"I can suppose anything. You know Mae. Maybe she lit out for somewhere. Well, since the blow-off can't run anyway, that'd save me money, for a change."

Late Tuesday afternoon it quit raining. But the sky stayed overcast and the lot, despite tons of shavings the cat-men were pushing around, stayed soggy even in the high spots. The lower areas were swamps.

Tuesday evening, a few intrepid suckers came out to see the carney. We opened up and I was out on the platform grinding all evening. We took in a little. Not enough to get off the nut, but it was less of a loss than if we hadn't worked at all.

Chapman helped plenty. Working to tips of only six or seven marks at a time inside the top, he'd get quarters away from almost a hundred percent of them.

Between grinds I asked him if anybody'd heard from Mae Cole.

"She's back," he said. "She's around somewhere. I saw her half an hour ago."

I didn't know whether that was good news or not. Anyway, it was time for another bally out front, so I took Bugs and the colonel and hammered the bass drum until I had the nearest thing to a crowd I'd be likely to get. Colonel Toots did a cartwheel and a headstand for them, and Bugs showed them the long hatpins he was going to stick into himself inside the top, and I told 'em about the myriad other wonders of the Wonderworld.

Three of them bought tickets and the rest wandered off. I kept on grinding. By eleven o'clock we had all we were going to get, and there wasn't any use keeping on.

Stella and I went up the midway for coffee and on our way back met Bugs Cartier heading out for the entrance.

He waved cheerfully. "Come on, you two," he yelled, "help me get drunk to celebrate."

"Celebrate what?" Stella asked him.

"Getting rich. Look!" He pulled some bills from his pockets. There were five or six of them; the one on top was a five. He held them up gleefully. "I broke the bank at Monte Cristo."

"Monte Carlo," I corrected him.

"All right then, Monte Carlo. Who cares? Let's go in town and get pie-eyed. On me."

"Don't tempt me," I told him, "because tomorrow gives the inquest. Up early we get."

"O.K., be a dope and be sensible." He grinned. "Me, I'm gonna have fun."

"Seriously, Bugs, where'd you get all that sugar?"

He put his finger to his lips and said, "Shhh!" And then he walked on and left us standing there. I got a whiff of his breath as he went by—he'd already been drinking.

Stella and I went on more slowly. I said, "I . . . I wonder where Bugs got that dough."

"The G-top? He gambles there a lot, doesn't he?"

"For peanuts. I've never seen him lose or win more than two or three bucks at a time. And he's been working up to half an hour ago. Dammit, I wish—"

"What, Pete?"

"I should have gone with the guy to keep him out of trouble. Somebody'll roll him, if nothing worse. He hasn't got sense enough, even when he's sober, not to stick pins in himself."

"Hm-m-m—I wish you wouldn't, Pete. You . . . you might get in trouble yourself."

That, from Stella, was encouraging. I said, "Would you care if I did?"

She said, "Well —" But never finished it, because I was looking at her instead of where I was going, and I stepped into a mudhole, and that was an end to romance.

Stella's laughter, after she made sure I wasn't hurt, destroyed the opportunity, and anyway you can't make love to a girl when you're coated with mud. I scraped off as much of it as I could and then took Stella to her car.

"Up early," I warned her. "The stars are coming out, and that means good weather tomorrow, maybe. If we can get back from Haverton by early afternoon —"

When I left Stella, regardless of the mud I was caked with, I headed for the G-top. Ralph Chapman, Gus Smith, and Shorty O'Hara were there, in a poker game with a couple of the ride men.

Shorty O'Hara — who doubles swords and fire for the freak show — had thrown in his cards, and Ralph and Gus were eying one another warily over a pot that had grown to several dollars. So I asked Shorty, "Seen Bugs?"

"No," he said. "What happened to you?"

"Beauty treatment," I told him. "You've heard of mud packs, haven't you? Was Bugs here at all this evening?"

O'Hara shook his head. "Nope, and I came here as soon as we closed. I asked Bugs then, was he coming, and he said no, he was going to see Lee."

I left the G-top more curious than before. Had Bugs hit Lee for an advance? Didn't seem likely, under the circumstances. And yet where else could Bugs have got that money in so short a time?

There wasn't any light in Lee's trailer, and I went on back to the sleeping car. Tomorrow, I decided. I'd pin Bugs down — and then the idea of pinning down a pincushion made me laugh out loud.

Slim Norris, the ticket man, stuck his head out of the upper bunk over mine and wanted to know what was funny.

I told him and asked him if he'd noticed what Bugs had done after the show.

"Dunno, Pete," he said, "but he didn't dip into the receipts. I checked in with Lee right after eleven. Took in only seventeen bucks. Lousy."

But after I was in bed I stopped worrying about it and went to sleep. Wednesday morning was bright and sunny. It was Lieutenant Helsing who awakened me, and he wasn't gentle about it.

"Wake up, you mug. Lee wants to get an early start. Gonna be a swell day."

I sat on the edge of the bunk and started pulling on my socks. "You're getting the carney spirit," I said, "because you're finding out what weather is. Sunshine is money and rain is a kick in the pants."

Helsing grinned. "Shake a leg, then. There's enough money outside to sunburn a lifeguard."

Then his voice turned serious. He said, "Pete you carneys stick together, don't you? And the rest of us are outsiders."

"Hm-m-m — yeah, we do. It's . . . it's kind of a world in itself, a world against the world."

"Look, Pete, here's what I want to know. How far would a carney go — to protect another one? I mean, if you knew somebody with this show had committed murder, would you — uh — perjure yourself at the inquest? Wait, I'll make that easier — let's say you don't *know* who did it, but you could tell something that would maybe be a lead for the police. Would you?"

"That's a tough one," I said. And I stopped to think, so I could give him an honest answer.

Then I said, "I guess a lot would depend on who it was, and what the circumstances were, and stuff like that. Maybe, in some cases, I might keep my yap shut. Like if it happened in a fight, and the guy hadn't meant to kill the other one. But then again —"

"It wasn't in a fight," Helsing interrupted. "Al Hryner was hit from the back. And a blow that hard was deliberate murder."

I stopped buttoning my shirt and stared at him. I said, "I

wasn't talking about Hryner. I was trying to give you a general answer to a general question, and to be fair about it. I don't know anything about the Hryner business I haven't told."

Helsing said, "O.K., don't get your back up. What I'm getting at is that *somebody* with this show—and I don't mean the murderer—must have *some* idea of what happened. Hell, we haven't even found a motive—except the ones I accused you of, once. Nobody will even admit knowing Hryner very well, and we can't find what outfit he was with before he joined your show."

"Lee hired him. Did you ask Lee?"

"Yeah, he says he didn't even ask the guy. You carneys are casual as the devil about stuff like that. How'd he even know the guy was a carney."

"He could tell."

"Hm-m-m," said Helsing. "By the way, you had a fortuneteller with the show in Haverton. What happened to him?"

I grinned. "That's what I meant about a carney being able to tell another carney. If you knew the lingo you'd have asked if the law sloughed the mitt camp. They did."

"Why the mitt camp?"

"Mitt for hand; mitt camp is a palmistry booth. But in carney it's stretched to cover any mentalist act. Hassan Bey pitches buddha."

And I had to translate that for him while we crossed the lot from the bunk car to Lee's trailer. Lee was looking over a list Helsing had given him of those who would have to go over to Haverton to give testimony at the inquest.

"We'll need two cars," he told me. "I'll unhitch mine from the trailer and Gus Smith can take his. You and Helsing ride with Gus and I can manage the rest. Better go tell Gus. And where the devil is Bugs?"

"Huh? Isn't he around?" I'd plumb forgotten about Bugs going into town to get drunk last night.

"I looked inside the top when I got up this morning," Lee said. "Bugs' bedroll was put away, so I figured he was up and around the lot somewhere."

"Damn," I said. "More likely it means he didn't get back last night." And I told Lee and Helsing about my encounter with Bugs the night before.

Lee whistled. He said, "I didn't give him any money last night. But if he had some he probably ended up in the Wilmot jail. You go see Gus, Pete, while I go to the pay wagon and phone the hoosegow."

He hightailed off toward the phone and I wandered into the waxworks tent to look for Gus. Gus has one end of the big tent partitioned off into living quarters and a workshop.

I found him making coffee on a primus stove and had a cup with him while I told him about arrangements for going over to Haverton.

He said, "Let's see if Lee found Bugs. Might put a crimp in the plans if one of us has to pick him up somewhere. Where's Lee now?"

I put down my coffee cup and stood. "Back at the trailer, I guess. That's base of operations. Let's see if he found out anything."

We ducked under the side wall and saw there was a knot of people by the trailer. Shorty O'Hara was there, and Ralph Chapman, and Stella, besides Helsing and Lee.

"Of course I'm sure, dammit," Shorty was saying. "No, I don't know what time it was, but I'd guess around three."

Lee saw me join the edge of the group and explained, his face looking worried. "Pete, Shorty here saw Bugs come back last night. He isn't in the hoosegow. I can't figure it out. How tight was he, Shorty?"

"Plenty. He could barely navigate."

Lee said, "Then he sure as shooting wouldn't have been in

the mood to get up early this morning. Not if he turned in with a snoot full like that—"

"Where does he keep his bedroll," I asked, "when he isn't in it?"

Lee jerked his thumb toward a wagon back of us.

Chapman said, "I know where he keeps it. I'll go look."

He was back in a minute. "'Bugs' bedding isn't there. But, dammit, he isn't on his platform, and that's where he sleeps, isn't it?"

Lee snapped his fingers. "Why didn't somebody think of it? Sometimes he sleeps on the cooch stage in the blow. Go look there, will you, Slim?"

Slim Norris ducked under canvas into the blow-off.

A minute later he reappeared, his face a pasty gray. He was looking mostly at me and there was something I didn't like in his expression.

He said, "The guy's dead."

Helsing and Chapman were running for the canvas. Some of the others followed, more slowly, and Lee sat down suddenly on the trailer step behind him.

His face looked suddenly old, as though the courage had gone out of it. He said, "Slim, was he—"

Slim said, "Yeah," in answer to Lee's unasked question, but Slim was looking at me. He said, "Pete, he was murdered just like you thought'd be funny." I was starting toward the tent, but I turned.

"Huh?" I grabbed Slim's arm. "What you acting funny about, Slim? Like you think *I* killed him or something, and saying— What you mean 'like I thought'd be funny'?"

"Last night." Slim's face was sullen and so was his voice. "You laughed at the idea of somebody pinning down a pincushion."

"Pinning? You mean—"

But what was the use of trying to get the story out of Slim? I let go his arm and went after the others into the top and slid through the slit in the canvas partition that shut off the blow end of the tent.

The curtains of the cooch stage had been pulled shut, but Helsing was holding them apart, and some of the others were crowding around him. I ran up and looked over Helsing's shoulder.

Bugs was dead, all right. He had to be, with a dozen six and nine-inch hatpins stuck into him that way. And one of them embedded so deeply that only the head showed, just above where his heart would be.

Chapter V: "Who Is Next?"

Helsing had phoned and we sat around waiting for the Wilmot police to get there. Waiting for the inevitable questioning, the inevitable bulldozing we knew we were in for.

None of us talked much.

Lee asked Helsing about the inquest at Haverton.

"I phoned there," Helsing told him, "and it's postponed. Seton will want to do his work here while this is fresh."

"I suppose we don't work today at all," said Chapman bitterly.

Helsing shrugged. "That'll be up to Seton. This is out of my territory."

But from the tone of his voice, and what we'd seen of William L. Seton, all of us knew the answer to Chapman's question. We'd be lucky to get going at all this week. Two inquests to worry about now instead of one.

The Wilmot chief of police brought the coroner and half a dozen policemen with him when he arrived. The coroner immediately took charge of the blow-off part of the top and Seton — with a black look on his face that boded trouble — herded the rest of us into the main part.

He said to a couple of his men, "Tommy, you and George keep an eye on these people. Nobody to go anywhere unless I know about it. Now, which one of you people knows the most about this?"

Nobody spoke up while he glared around at all of us.

Lee said quietly, "Slim Norris found the body when I sent him to look on the cooch stage. Maybe you'll want to talk to Slim first."

"Why'd you send him to look there?"

Lee explained.

"All right. If you don't mind I'll use your trailer. Come on, Norris."

Stella was sitting alone on the tin trunk that still contained two of the snakes. I climbed the platform and sat down beside her. I said, "Don't worry, kid. This'll come out all right."

"But, Pete, who'll be next?"

"Next?" I stared at her, wondering what she meant. And then I got it. "Good Lord, don't get ideas like that. You think somebody's going to bump off the freak show, one at a time?"

"It . . . it sounds silly, Pete, but isn't that what's happening? Three already!"

"*Three?*" I echoed, and for a minute I thought either she or I had gone loco, and then I got what she meant. "Oh, Black King. But, in all probability, honey, he just ran off. There are woods not far from here, and —"

"You think he opened the trunk himself, from the inside? Don't be silly, Pete. Black King was murdered."

"Humph," I said. "Why would anyone do a screwy thing like that?"

"For the same reason they . . . he . . . killed Bugs last night. And Al last week. Don't you see it, Pete? Somebody's trying to break up the show."

It was so silly I couldn't help grinning. I said, "Anybody who would try to break up a freak show by murdering the acts one at a time would — Hey, Al Hryner wasn't even an act! Murdering a canvasman would be a funny way to start a campaign like that. They'd pick somebody valuable, like —"

I'd started to say "like you," but I stopped, because the idea of anybody murdering Stella wasn't anything I wanted to talk about. Suddenly I was afraid for her.

Two people who'd been with the show *had* been murdered, and as long as I didn't know why they'd died, who was I to say that the motive might not extend to Stella?

I happened to be looking at the canvas partition of the blow-off when I saw what had been the rosy, cherubic face of the coroner poke through the opening. But just then his face was neither rosy nor cherubic at all. There was an expression on it I couldn't read, further to say that it didn't indicate a pleasant emotion.

He called out, "Mr. Werner!"

I said, "Scuse me a minute," to Stella and got there the same time Lee did. Just curiosity as to what caused that expression. It couldn't be the manner in which Bugs had been killed, because he'd been in there ten or fifteen minutes, and the pins were obvious.

He said, "Come in a minute, Mr. Werner."

Neither of them paid any attention to me, and I followed through the flap. I was glad to see that the coroner had thrown the blanket up over the body of the pincushion. He'd taken out the hatpins, too; they were lying in a neat row along the footlights of the cooch stage.

He pointed to something I couldn't see, something lying beyond the blanket-covered body, and said to Lee, "Is — uh — that yours?"

I stepped in close when Lee did and saw what was lying there. A big black snake. Black King. And I could tell by the way he lay there, belly up, that he was dead. A live snake never lies that way, nor a sleeping one.

I heard Lee's breath suck in quickly. He said, "Yes, Doc, that's my snake. It . . . it disappeared night before last. We thought it just got away into the woods."

"How was it killed?" I asked.

The coroner shook his head. "Don't ask me. I'm no herpetologist. I dunno whether I could tell or not, even if I examined it." And by the expression in his eyes I could see that he wasn't keen about finding out.

"Where'd you find it?" Lee demanded.

"Partly alongside, partly under the body. Inside the bedroll. Did — did the deceased — uh — ever sleep with it?"

I shook my head slowly, remembering that Bugs Cartier hadn't liked snakes. He hadn't been exactly afraid of them, but he wouldn't have touched one voluntarily.

I said, "If it had been Bugs who stole Black King, the last place he'd have hidden him would have been in his own bedroll. Whether the snake was dead or alive at the time. And no matter how drunk Bugs was."

"He wasn't drunk the night Black King disappeared," Lee said. "Dammit, Pete —" Whatever he'd intended to say to me, he stopped, and turned to the coroner again. He asked, "About what time would you say Cartier was killed?"

"At least four hours ago, maybe longer. Say between three and six o'clock."

"Will a regular autopsy bring it out closer than that?"

"Maybe. Maybe not. Depends on whether his movements before then can be traced."

Lee looked puzzled. "I don't get it, Doc. How would his movements before three prove what time after that he was killed?"

"Contents of the stomach and esophagus. An analyst can show just about how long the last food he'd eaten had been there and progressed in digestion at the time of death. Then, if tracing his movements can show pretty accurately when it was that he ate the food in question, we can estimate the time of death pretty closely."

"Oh," said Lee. "I've often wondered about that."

As Lee and I went back into the main part of the top I asked him, "What made you so interested in time of death, Lee? Shorty saw him at three last night, and Slim found him about nine this morning. What good would it do to know whether he was killed at, say, three thirty or at six?"

"Guess I didn't have any real reason, Pete. I was thinking about that snake. It . . . it worries me. *Why* would anybody have put that snake in Bugs' bedroll?"

"That's less important than why somebody murdered Bugs."

"I . . . I don't know why, but one worries me more than the other, Pete. Because it seems so utterly unreasonable. If somebody had a reason for killing Al Hryner, maybe Bugs found out something about it. Maybe he was bribed last night to keep his mouth shut. Remember that money you told me about. But after Bugs got drunk, the killer decided he couldn't trust Bugs — and I can see why he'd decide that, after the way Bugs flashed the dough. So he waits till Bugs turns in, dead drunk, and —"

I nodded. "I see what you mean, Lee. That part of it can make sense, but the Black King part — it scares me a little."

And then I forgot about being scared, because it was up to me to break the news to Stella about her pet. But she took it better than I'd feared she might.

"I . . . I had a hunch, Pete, all along, that King was dead." Her voice was quite steady. "I . . . I'd rather not see him, I guess. But will you see that . . . that —"

"Sure, honey," I assured her. "I'll see he gets a decent burial."

And, I decided, he would. The police might think me crazy to insist on the point, but a pet is a pet, and Stella had thought at least as much of King as a man thinks of his dog.

Then Slim came under the side wall and crossed the tent to where I was talking to Stella. He said, "You're next, Pete."

There was still that look in his eyes as though he was afraid of me.

Chief Seton had put up the little folding table in Lee's trailer. He sat on one side of it, facing me, and a patrolman with a notebook sat at the end, taking notes. Presumably, I was supposed to stand for the inquisition, but I sat down on Lee's bed instead.

Seton started by frowning at me for what seemed like a full minute. There were several things that it occurred to me to say, but I waited. I was going to let him ask the questions.

When he started it was with the air of a man who is going to be very thorough.

"Your name?"

"Pete Gaynor. Peter John Gaynor."

"Age?"

"Thirty-six."

"Draft status?"

"Four-F. They wouldn't even let me enlist for noncombatant. I'm slightly hemophiliac."

"What's that?"

"In a way, sort of the opposite of whatever it was made Bugs Cartier into a human pincushion. A hemophiliac is a person whose blood won't clot properly. An extreme case can bleed to death from a pin prick. I'm not that bad, but I've got to be very careful; even a slight scratch can be dangerous to me."

Seton nodded. "I've heard of that, but I didn't recognize the name. Was Cartier's act on the level, or was there any trick about it?"

"There wasn't any gaff. He could stick pins into himself without it hurting, or without bleeding. Not straight in, of course. He just stuck them under the skin, ran them along parallel to the surface, and then out again. Like a needle through cloth."

"He didn't feel it?"

"Not much anyway. It used to give me the willies to watch him do it, though. He'd even take a needle and thread and sew buttons on himself."

"You think he wouldn't have felt it when — uh — somebody stuck those needles into him last night?"

"I've been thinking about that," I said. "I think he would have. His insensitivity was just surface, just his skin. But don't forget, first that he was dead drunk, and second, that if that one through his heart was the first one in, he wouldn't have had a chance to feel the others. That's the way I figure it happened."

"How many people knew he sometimes slept on the stage in the end compartment of the tent?"

"I guess anybody with the show could have known it," I said. "I don't know just which ones did."

"You figure it this way, Gaynor? After he's asleep somebody peels back the blanket and jabs the pin into his heart, and then sticks the others in?"

"It must have been that way. Unless the first one was the fatal one, it would have awakened him, drunk or not. The pins, by the way, look like the ones Bugs used in his act. I think you'll find they were. He used about a dozen of them."

"All at once?"

I shook my head. "Never saw him use more than three at once, but he carried a battery of them for flash."

"And the snake? Berger, the coroner, was just in here and told me about it. How do you figure a dead snake figures in this?"

"I don't," I told him honestly. "I can't even make an intelligent guess about that. But I can tell you when it disappeared, and how."

He listened intently while I told him about the episode of the night before last. I expected a storm and felt relieved when all he said was, "You should have reported it. Do you think that whoever it was knocked the flash out of your hand stole the snake — or just opened the box?"

"I wouldn't even guess. But I'll tell you one thing. The snake didn't crawl into Bugs' bedroll then because he got back in afterward. He'd have felt it. He sleeps in nothing but a pair of shorts — as you found him this morning."

"Hm-m-m," said Seton. "Then you think it was put there, in his bedroll, I mean, *after* he was killed?"

I thought that over a minute before I answered. "Not necessarily," I told him. "If he was as drunk as I think he was when he turned in, it might have been there without his knowing about it."

Seton said, "Getting back to the stealing of the snake, could it have been handled by anybody? Anybody with the carnival, I mean."

"Sure. King was tame and harmless. Wait — I can eliminate one. Ralph Chapman, the magician. He has a horror of snakes and wouldn't have gone near one on a bet. He has what's practically a phobia about snakes."

"But anybody else might have?"

"As far as I know. Most of us have a normal dislike of touching snakes, I guess, but not enough of an aversion to keep us from picking one up if we had an important reason. Only —"

"Only what?"

"Only *damned* if I can figure any reason why anybody, with the carney or otherwise, would have stolen and killed King and put him in Bugs' bedroll. Just doesn't make sense."

"How valuable was this Black King?"

I said, "Not enough for that to be much of a factor. Less than a hundred bucks, anyway."

Seton sighed. He took a cigar from his pocket and bit off the end. He said, "This is a hell of a case. Let's get back to you. How long did you know Cartier?"

"Bugs joined the carney the middle of last season. That was the first time I ever saw him. He's been with some little outfit out on the West coast."

"How did he get with Tookerman Shows?"

"Lee hired him through Bugs' ad in *Billboard*. The carney he was with out there folded, and he stuck an At Liberty ad in the wanteds."

"Know anything about his affairs, his relations with other people around here?"

"He hadn't any enemies I know of," I said. "Kind of a good-natured screwball. Nobody took him very seriously."

"Until last night," said Seton dryly. "Norris, by the way, told me Bugs flashed a roll last night. Tell me what you know about that."

I told him.

Seton asked, "He could have won it gambling?"

I said, "I don't think it likely. It was big money for Bugs; he seldom shot more than a dime or a quarter at a time and, at that rate, he wouldn't have had time enough to run it up to real folding money. It was too shortly after closing. Was there any money in his clothes when you examined them?"

"Not a cent. He might have spent it all or been rolled while he was off the lot, but —"

Seton nodded. "But it's more likely the killer took it. Maybe — took it back."

That talk with Seton made me feel better about things. Helsing was a good guy, but he hadn't shown any streaks of brilliance. I was putting my money on Seton now.

Funny, I thought; twice in two weeks now I'd scratched a copper and found a decent guy under the blue.

Or was Seton just stringing us along? It seemed not, for by two o'clock in the afternoon he told us we could go ahead and open.

We opened, but the crowds were thin that afternoon on the midway. Everybody seemed to work in a desultory way, as if they were waiting for something, not knowing quite what. Colonel Toots was in one of his black, cantankerous moods. He wouldn't put any oomph into the bally.

I did my best to turn the scanty tips, but the percentage wasn't good. It wasn't even fair. If the crowd that afternoon was representative, then Wilmot was going to be a tough town. I wanted to talk it over with Lee to see if he could suggest any way to pep up the percentage; but Lee had gone in to town with Seton, and would probably be gone most of the day.

After a while, during a time when the only marks in front of the platform were ones who'd been there a long time and apparently had no intention of going farther, I told Slim to hold down the fort and strolled inside.

Ralph was just finishing his spiel. He had a small tip and made no sales. Disgustedly, he directed them across the tent to listen to the colonel, and came to join me at the ridge pole.

"They're dead, Pete, all of them. Not a live one in this town. I dropped from two bits to a dime and didn't sell any anyway, so I put the price back up. Haven't taken in two bucks all afternoon. What do they want for two bits?"

"Maybe they want Mae Cole," I told him. "Say, did she get to first base with Seton?"

"Don't know. But, hell, if she did, it'd be out now. We're going to have coppers on our necks all the time we're here. I can't work with John Law watching every move. I even dropped a card on the monte."

He stared sourly at the policeman leaning against the opposite ridge pole, who was staring sourly in turn at Bessie, the fat woman. Bessie wasn't staring at anything; she'd gone to sleep.

Ralph chuckled. "The spirit of Wilmot. What a town. For ten lousy cents I'd chuck it and head for Florida. I can play the night clubs there, and there's only three weeks of Tookerman left anyhow."

"That would be a dirty trick on Lee," I said. "He's on the nut. He needs two weeks of gravy to get set for the winter. And Lord, Ralph, you're the only inside money he's getting."

"Nuts," said Ralph. "He won't even get peanuts on his percentage of me, if the rest of this week is like today. And lookit, Pete, there's another reason for scramming. *Who's next?*"

"What you mean?"

"You know what I mean. Al and Bugs. And then maybe you, maybe me, maybe Stella."

I felt something start to boil up inside me and I choked it down. Suddenly—for mentioning Stella that way—I wanted to take a poke at the guy. But if he was on the verge of leaving us like a rat deserting a sinking ship, a poke would be all he needed to make it sure.

I said, "That's silly. Why would anybody kill one of us?"

"Why did somebody kill Al and Bugs?"

"Probably somebody had a reason for killing Al. And the same guy killed Bugs because he found out something he shouldn't have. That won't apply to any of the others of us—at least without our knowing about it."

Yes, I choked down my anger and made myself reason with him. I could call him a rat, or yellow, but that wouldn't help Lee any.

He took a half dollar out of his pocket and it twinkled between his fingers as he back and front palmed it while he talked. He said quietly, "And Black King. Did he know too much?"

There wasn't any answer to that, not any that I could think of at the moment, so I didn't say anything.

The half dollar twinkled a moment and then was gone. Ralph turned his hand backward and forward as though looking for it, and then spread his fingers apart.

He said, "You think I'm a louse, don't you, Pete?"

A minute ago, I had. But it's hard to answer yes when a guy asks you that, quietly and calmly.

I said, "I . . . I wouldn't put it that strongly, Ralph. But, dammit, if you walk out on Lee—"

He nodded. "Come on back to the wagon. I want to show you something. Then maybe you won't think I'm talking through my hat."

Chapter VI: "You Can't Quit Now!"

I said, "Wait a minute," and went out front again. There was a bally going on in front of the girl show and nearly all the people on our end of the midway were over there. It wouldn't hurt to be gone another fifteen minutes or so.

Slim grinned at me. "Can I sell you a ticket, mister?"

"I'll be gone fifteen or twenty minutes, Slim," I told him. "If you want to shut the gate and get yourself a mug of java, go ahead."

"Swell. Help me stay awake, through all this rush of business."

I went back to Ralph and we went under the side wall and back to the big red wagon back of Lee's trailer. I knew Ralph kept his trunk and his bedding there, and slept there. Bugs kept his stuff there, too, but always slept in the top.

I quit trying to guess what Ralph was going to show me, and just followed him as he climbed into the wagon. He crossed over to the roll of bedding and unrolled it, then lifted the top blanket carefully.

I said, "What's the —"

And then the blanket went back farther, and I saw what was lying on the bedding under the center of it. I started to laugh, and the laughter stuck in my throat, because maybe it was as far from funny as anything I'd ever seen.

It was a toy snake, about a foot long, painted bright green and yellow and made up of jointed wooden segments. I recognized it as having come from the marble-game concession up at the front end of the midway. Curley Bates, who ran marbles, had a dozen of them among his flash.

Ralph said, "Somebody put it there this morning. It wasn't there last night."

"But why —"

"I can't even guess," Ralph said. I noticed that his eyes were on me, and not on the toy, and that there were slight beads of sweat on his forehead.

He said, "Uh — Take it, will you, Pete. I . . . I just can't make myself touch the damn thing. It's silly, yes, and I know it's not a real snake and just a toy, but . . . but I *can't.*"

I said, "Sure, Ralph." I picked it up and it wriggled quite realistically as I turned my hand. Then I caught a glimpse of Ralph's face, and stuffed the toy out of sight into my pocket. I know what a phobia is; I'd known phobiacs before.

I asked, "How do you know it was put there this morning? How'd you happen to find it?"

"It *wasn't* there last night. And about noon when I came back to get my sleeve-pull, I noticed that my bedroll didn't look the way I'd left it. I always have the edges neat. I wondered who'd messed with it, and I opened it out to roll it again."

He was rolling it again, neatly, while he talked. I leaned against the side wall of the wagon, my hand still in my pocket and touching the toy snake, and — I began to get scared.

I don't know why. There'd been two murders within a week, and *they* didn't scare me. But there'd been two things that were outwardly much less important than murders, and they *did* scare me. The business about Black King, and now this about the toy snake.

Murder, a man can understand. It's something he doesn't understand that can give him the screaming meamies.

Ralph was lighting a cigarette and his hand shook a little. He said, "I got to leave, Pete."

Well, I had to talk him out of that again. I said, "Don't be a dope, Ralph. Just because somebody plays a joke —" I couldn't quite finish it convincingly, because anybody who understood Ralph's abnormal fear of snakes wouldn't consider that a joke.

Ralph said, "How'd you go for a drink?" And before I answered, he opened his trunk beside the bedroll and pulled out a bottle and a shot glass. He poured some in the glass, spilling a little of it, and handed it to me.

"I'll drink out of the bottle, Pete. Listen, I know why somebody put that there. The toy snake, I mean."

"Why?"

"To let me know what they'd intended to do. What they missed doing. See?"

I didn't. I didn't get it at all, and while I was thinking it over I tossed down the whiskey. Then I asked what he meant.

"Black King. He got put in Bugs' bedroll by mistake—he was meant for mine! Last night somebody put him in Bugs' bedding by mistake, Pete. And this morning they put that . . . that toy in there to let me know what I'd missed. To give me something to think about."

"But that's—" I couldn't quite say it was crazy, because it made a kind of sense. If somebody was deliberately trying to scare Ralph Chapman that somebody was succeeding. His face was a yellowish white—just from *thinking* how close he had come to getting into bed with a seven-foot snake.

Yes, it would have been a dead snake, and even if it were alive it wouldn't have hurt him, but things like that carry no weight against the blinding unreasoning fear that is phobia. Feeling a big, real snake in close contact with him in the dark—whether that snake was alive or dead—would have probably sent Ralph to a sanitarium. Even thinking about it was doing him a lot of no good.

And, understanding how he felt, I couldn't blame the guy, but—

"Ralph," I said, "you *got* to stick it out. Man, you're a trouper; you aren't going to let something scare you into ratting on the show only a few weeks from close."

"But maybe next time it won't be a toy!"

"Phooey." I spoke with a confidence I was far from feeling.

"Hey, I got an idea. How's the weasel sack?"

"I got money. Not a lot, but—"

"Look, I know how you feel, after finding that thing, and I don't blame you. But there's an easy out. There are a couple of houses that have furnished rooms to rent within a few blocks of the lot here. For anyway the rest of our stay in Wilmot, why don't you take a furnished room instead of sleeping here? Cost you only a few bucks, and maybe it'd do you good to pretend you're civilized for a while anyway. Get used to sleeping in a bed before you hit the night-club circuit."

"Pete, that's an idea." There was what seemed to be genuine gratitude in Ralph's eyes, and I knew I'd hit the answer. "Pete, it isn't the days—but I just couldn't face going to sleep here. Wondering who might—hell, there isn't even any way you can lock this wagon from the inside. Have another drink on that!"

"Sure." I held out my glass while he poured a stiffer one than the first.

"I . . . I got rattled, Pete. I should've thought of that answer myself. I don't *want* to rat on Lee if I can keep from it. Even if—"

"If what?"

He hesitated. "Maybe I should have kept my yap shut about this, Pete. Because I'm not sure. But—"

"Get it off your chest. But what?"

"I think Lee owed money to Al Hryner."

I whistled softly. *"Lee* owing money to a canvasman? Hell, Ralph, Lee pays salaries on the dot, and if he covers the others why would he have held out on a canvasman's lousy few bucks? Or— Wait a minute, do you mean gambling?"

For suddenly I remembered Helsing's telling me that the dice he'd found in Al Hryner's pocket were crooked dice. And if Al had got Lee pyramiding in a crap game—but no, that didn't make sense either. Lee wasn't born yesterday, and he wouldn't have shot for big stakes with somebody else's crooked dice. Matter of fact,

Lee never gambled heavily anyway — with dice or cards. He didn't have to gamble that way — backing and running a freak show is enough of an odds-on bet for any man.

Chapman said, "It wasn't salary and I don't think it was gambling. I think Hryner had a stake and invested it with Lee."

"A stake? Hm-m-m — it doesn't quite make sense, Ralph. A canvasman having enough money to invest it with a big concession like this. Why, Lee's got ten to twenty thousand tied up in this show. More, come to think of it. Anyway, where'd you get the idea?"

"I heard them talking once, Pete. Didn't get all of it, but got the idea that Hryner had a couple hundred bucks when he came here and — well, it could have been that he gave it to Lee to keep for him, but I got the idea that if Lee could use it, he was going to pay it back with a bonus."

I thought it over and it could be. Lee was hard pressed for running capital lately. Still — "You sure it was only a couple hundred!" I asked.

"I thought Lee mentioned a couple of C's; it *could* have been a couple of G's instead. Which ever it was, Lee won't have to pay it back now. Don't get me wrong, Pete; I don't mean Lee would have killed Al for a couple of hundred bucks."

I grinned. "But you think for a couple of thousand, he might have."

Ralph didn't grin back. He said, "A couple of thousand is a lot of money. And Lee's having to borrow now anyway. He's running in debt to Tookerman, and to Gus Smith."

"Gus? Hell, I didn't think Gus would lend his own mother money."

Ralph said, "The way I get it, he's taking a lien on some of the physical property. The top and the platforms and banners and stuff."

"What would he do with that?" I wanted to know. "Does he

intend to run two shows next year? That is, if Lee can't square up?"

Ralph shook his head. "Gus was fair about that. He doesn't want two shows. He'd let Lee operate it next year and settle out of the profits. But until settlement, technical ownership would be Gus'— that is, the physical property, not the concession."

"Well, that's a fair enough arrangement," I said. "Say, we better get back. I'll put on one more bally and then grind awhile before the crowd goes home to eat."

By eight o'clock Lee still wasn't there. But the terror was starting.

It was something difficult to define, something you couldn't put your finger on. I know I felt it, and couldn't tell just why, or just what I was afraid of.

Maybe there's something to this business about mental telepathy and mass hysteria. It couldn't have been exactly telepathy, though, unless it was that the minds of everybody with the show were in tune with each other in some way that left outsiders on the outside. The marks didn't feel it. I watched them to see.

But there was a minute just before I was getting ready to start a bally, when I happened to look across the platform at Colonel Toots. There was terror in his strange little face.

His eyes caught mine and he motioned to me. I put down the mike and went over to him. He said, "Pete, I'm through. I'll stick out this evening."

Knowing I didn't have to ask, I asked anyway, "Why?"

"I don't want to be murdered!" His voice rose shrilly at the end of it; so much so that I gave a quick look out front to see if the suckers could hear us. But they couldn't, I guess.

I bent over so I wouldn't have to talk loudly. I said, "Don't get excited, colonel. There's nothing to worry—"

"The hell with you. I'm quitting, tonight. Before somebody cuts off my head."

"*Cuts off your head?* Where on earth do you get a wild idea like —"

"That's what they'd do to a midget, isn't it? To make him shorter! Don't you see it, you dope. How was Al Hryner killed?"

"With a tent stake. But what's that got to do with it?"

"He was a canvasman, wasn't he? Worked with tent stakes. And how'd they kill the pincushion? With pins. They took Stella's snake and I'll bet they were going to kill her with it. There's a crazy guy with this show, Pete. Well, he isn't going to get *me!* I'm —"

"Shut up," I said. "Colonel, you're working yourself up to a case of jitters. Can it. Think about something else, anyway till Lee gets back."

"Yeah, and where is Lee? Would he stay down at the station *this* long? I'll bet *he's* murdered, Pete. Right now he's lying out in a ditch somewhere with —"

Well, I wasn't getting anywhere with Colonel Toots, and by listening to him I was letting him talk himself into the screaming meamies.

I went over and hammered on the bass drum instead, and when I had a tip, or anyway the start of one, I picked up the mike and started to spiel.

After the next grind I pulled out Shorty and Stella for the bally instead of Colonel Toots.

Maybe I shouldn't have. It was Shorty's turn to pop off, and being out on the platform gave him a chance.

He said, "Listen, Pete, I think we better call off the knife throwing for tonight. Agnes is nervous."

"Nuts," I said. "Why should she be nervous? She knows by now you don't miss with those knives. And there's —"

"Sure, I don't miss. But — Grief, I know how she feels with everything that's been going on around here. Suppose somebody pulled something like changing the weighting in those throwing knives?"

"Don't be a dope. You could tell the minute you picked one up."

"Yeah, but something else then. Look, she's going to have a nervous breakdown or something if she keeps on flinching like she's been doing every time I throw one. She's a good trouper, but— Look, Pete, I'll go on swallowing swords and I'll stretch the act there. I'll hold 'em ten minutes instead of five, with the swords."

I said, "All right, all right. But you got to have Agnes around for flash. Have her on the platform with you and have her hand you the stuff you use instead of you taking it off the display board."

He grinned. "Atta boy, Pete. Then it won't matter what I do anyway. They'll watch Agnes' legs instead."

I was pretty thoughtful while I hammered the drum.

Pretty soon, at this rate, we just weren't going to have any show left. No pincushion. Maybe after tonight, no midget. The cooch blow and the mitt camp sloughed. Ralph ready to leave if somebody pushed an oversize worm at him.

Not so good. All we had left besides the colonel and Ralph was half of Shorty O'Hara's part in the show, Bessie Williams, and Stella. And Stella's good snake was gone; now she had only the two four-foot bull snakes to work with, and they didn't have the flash of Black King. Sure, Black King had been a bull, too, but he had flash. You could call him a blacksnake or a python or a constrictor, and get by with it.

When I finished ballying and turned all of the tip I could get inside the top, I strolled back to the entrance and watched inside for a while.

Ralph was doing his act, manipulating the cardboards. His voice sounded jerky and his movements were wooden—for a prestidigitator. The others, too, sat around listlessly. I noticed that Stella's face was utterly blank, and I wondered what went on behind it. Was she, too, sharing the fear that the rest of the performers felt so obviously? Well, I'd see her after close and find out.

Someone behind me said, "Mr. Gaynor?" I turned.

She was a blonde and she was beautiful, but she looked tough. You get used to tough dames in carney, but this one was tougher— if looks meant anything.

Rather warily, I admitted my name.

She said, "The guy at the ticket box said you could tell me where I'd find Lee Werner."

"Went to town this afternoon and isn't back yet. Anything I can do for you?"

"Uh—I guess not. I'll wait." She smiled brightly. "How goes the keeasarney?"

I said, "Oke," and tried to keep from frowning. She wasn't a carney or she wouldn't have used the carney double talk that way without reason. It's show-off outsiders who pop it casually, and carneys never use it unless they want to get something across over the heads of a tip. Outside carney, mostly chorines or chippies use it. This one could have been either—or both.

"He'll be back tonight, won't he?" she asked.

I said, "I think so. I better get back on the platform. You can wait here or look around inside."

"I'll look around inside."

She turned to go in, but just then I saw Lee coming, and I said, "Wait." And then, "Here he comes. How'll I introduce you?"

"Mrs. Hryner, Dotty Hryner. I was Al's wife."

Chapter VII: Mrs. Dotty Hryner

Lee wandered up, looking like a lost soul. He said, "Hi, Pete. How's business?"

"Lousy," I told him. "Lee, this is Dotty Hryner. Says she was Al's wife. Wants to see you."

And, because I was curious what she wanted to see him about, I stuck around.

Lee said, "I suppose your husband told you about the money, Mrs. Hryner?"

The blonde nodded. "He said a hundred and fifty."

"That's right," said Lee. "Or two hundred at the end of the season. He asked me to keep it for him and I could use it if I wanted. And I said I would, but in that case I'd give him back two hundred at the end of the season. Which way you want it?"

"Which way— I don't get it."

Lee grinned. "Sure, you get it. But you can have the hundred fifty right now, or if you want to wait a few weeks till the season's over, you get two hundred. But, of course, you can prove you're really Mrs. Hryner. I suppose you have something to prove that?"

She nodded again eagerly. "I got a letter Al sent me the week he joined up with you." She fished in her handbag, among some papers, and pulled out an envelope. She handed it to Lee and I stepped around to look over his shoulder.

The envelope was O.K. It had "Al Hryner, Tookerman Shows, c/o Billboard, Cincinnati, Ohio," as the return address. It was addressed to Dotty Wilbur, at an address in Chicago. Postmark was in August.

Dotty caught Lee's glance resting on the name. She said, "That's my maiden name. I was using it because I was with a show in Chi. I used my stage name, naturally."

Without comment, Lee took the single sheet of writing paper out of the envelope. The handwriting was the same as that on the envelope. The letter read:

> Dear Dotty: Joined up with Tookerman and I'm handling canvas for Lee Werner, who runs the freak show. The hundred and fifty bucks I had with me I gave to Lee to keep, because, neither of us needs it now. If anything should happen to me, you can get it from Lee.
>
> Doc B. did a swell job and I'm feeling great. Let me know if there's any change in your address or anything. I'll head for Chi at the end of the season and—

The page ended there, and there wasn't anything on the other side when Lee turned it over.

Dotty said, "I lost the rest of the letter. I kept that page because it had your name and address on it. It . . . it hasn't got Al's name on it, and I never thought about that part because I never thought I'd have to use it, see? But you can compare the handwriting with his name on your records, and —"

"That's all right," said Lee. "You want one-fifty now or two at the end of the season?"

"I — uh — it don't matter much. I can wait till the end of the season. Look, what I really want most is a job. I can cooch. I'm good."

Lee looked surprised. "Huh? Sorry, we got a cooch girl and, anyway —"

"Please, Mr. Werner. I know it's near the end of the season, but I've always wanted to get into a carney, like Al was. And getting on with you will give me a start, and next year — But that's thinking too far ahead. Look, why don't you have *two* cooch girls the rest of the season. I'll work for almost nothing. I —"

"Sorry," said Lee. "But —"

I tapped him gently on the shoulder to stop him. I said, "Mrs. Hryner, mind if I talk to Lee a minute alone? I got an idea how we might work you in."

She gave me a dazzling smile that might have swept me off my feet if I went for glamour blondes with too much make-up even for carney.

She said, "Go ahead, Mr. Gaynor. Theeasanks."

Lee winced and I grabbed his arm and pulled him across the tent before he said anything.

Back behind Bessie's backdrop, I said, "Listen, Lee, give her a job. I got a hunch."

He snorted. "That dame? Anyone who says —"

"Hold everything and listen, Lee. There's something screwy

about her. Theeasanks or not, she's got no legit reason for wanting a job with you. Anyway, not so bad she'd offer to work for almost nothing. Don't let her walk off till we find out what makes her tick. Do you really think she's Al's wife?"

"His wife or something. That letter was on the up-and-up. I recognized Al's writing. And I do owe that dough. Only I'd rather she'd take the one-fifty and get the hell out of—"

"Shut up," I said. "Listen, we *can* use her. Shorty's wife's got the jitters and won't let him throw shivs at her. I had to tell him O.K., to leave out the throwing routine and stick to swallowing. You know how much that cuts the show, when it's cut already without the blow and without Hassan Bey and without Bugs—"

"Why didn't you tell me? Dammit, Agnes ought to—"

"Don't blame Agnes. Listen, I know how she feels and so do the rest of us. Right now *I* wouldn't let anybody around here throw knives at me for a million bucks a throw."

"*You,* yeah. You're a bleeder. But, dammit, Shorty's her husband. I got a mind to—"

"You got a mind to break up the show? Ralph's on the verge of quitting. The colonel's quit already, but I think you can talk him out of it if you fix things up so he can sleep in a room somewhere instead of on the lot. Now if this dame's willing to take Agnes' spot, and do it for peanuts, what you got to lose?"

"Hm-m-m," said Lee. It was a disgusted-sounding grunt, but I knew he was beginning to see reason.

"Look," I said, "for a few days anyway, until we find out what's what. Tell her you'll try her out on cooch later, but there's no cooch in Wilmot and if she wants to stand in for the knife-thrower while she's waiting, you're killing three birds with one stone. For free."

"Hm-m-m," said Lee. "Guess she's about the right size to wear that costume of Agnes'. Wonder if she's got legs."

"She's a chorine. She must have legs, especially if she wants to cooch. Whyn't you ask her to show you?"

And then before I oversold my product, I said, "I better get back for a bally out front. After you look at her legs, don't forget to soap up the colonel about quitting tonight. And listen, better mention casually to Ralph that you're giving Al's wife the money you owed Al."

"Huh? Why?"

"It'll take a load off his mind, and he's got several. Including this dingus he found in his bed today."

I pulled the toy snake partly out of my pocket so he could see it, and then stuffed it back in before anybody else could notice.

Lee whistled. "Who the hell would have put that in Ralph's bed?"

"There wasn't a card with it," I told him. "Not even 'Compliments of a Friend.' Better see Dotty before she decides we're calling copper on her and lams."

I went back to the platform and worked awhile.

A couple of ballys later, I yelled for swords, and Shorty came out. But he had his throwing knives with him and Dotty was trailing along after, wearing one of Agnes' costumes. She had gams, all right. If it wasn't for the hardness of her face she'd have been beautiful. Maybe she was, anyway; being in love with Stella I wasn't a judge.

Shorty O'Hara was smiling at Dotty and that meant, unless I missed my guess, that Agnes would pretty darned soon snap out of her jitters and be back in front of the knife board again. By tomorrow at the latest, and sooner if she got a good look at Dotty.

Crowds began to taper off around eleven, and I took time out to walk up to the marble-roll concession. I showed the toy snake to Curley and asked him if it had come from his booth.

He shrugged. "Could have, Pete. I passed out half a dozen of them last week."

I said, "I found this inside a wagon, where a mark couldn't

have dropped it. How about the carneys—any of them buy or win one of these from you?"

"No. What you worrying about it for? They cost only four forty a gross."

"It isn't the initial cost, Curley," I told him. "It's the upkeep." And leaving him puzzling over that I went back to the freak show. I hadn't really expected to find out anything, because whoever had put the snake in Ralph Chapman's bed wouldn't have obtained it openly.

By twelve things had tapered off enough that Lee told me to knock off. I took in the mike and the bass drum, and then hung around until the final tip had moved on past Stella's act. Then I took her to the chow top for coffee and.

"Pete," she said while we were waiting for Hank to bring on the doughnuts, "did you notice how everyone was feeling tonight? I'm wondering how long—"

I nodded. "Everybody's scared stiff, honey. Even me. How about you?"

"I . . . I guess I'm scared, too, Pete. It's awful to feel that way, and not to know just what you're scared about. Who is the girl taking Agnes' place, Pete? I . . . I don't think I'm going to like her."

I told her about Dotty, and some of my reasons for wanting her to be with the show for a while.

Stella said, "But, Pete aren't you sticking your own neck out? You think having her here may bring—things to a head, but you don't even know what you mean by 'things.' You're groping in the dark."

"Sure, but if you grope long enough in the dark you're bound to catch hold of *something*. It's sitting with your hands in your pockets that gets you nowhere fast."

"But it isn't your job, Pete, to find out what's going on. The police—"

"The police are trying, but they aren't getting anywhere. And, meanwhile, Lee's show is heading for the rocks. I hate to see Lee end up the season with a deficit and not even own the props he'll have to start out with next year. Sure, Gus'll let him run the show and pay back out of the profits, but it's hell to start way behind the nut."

My hand was lying on the table and she put hers over it. She said, "You're a good guy, Pete. If you would —"

"Hold the ifs," I said. "Stick to that I'm a good guy. Good enough to marry, even?"

"If you — Pete, why can't or won't you save your money?"

"What money?" I wanted to know. And then when I saw her face change, I said, "Aw, now, Stella. I was only kidding. Matter of fact, I have got a little ahead, and I've put it where I can't get at it easily and that's why I've been broke a lot recently. Won't you —"

"Where? What did you do with the money?"

"Now listen, Stella, a guy's got a right to —"

"Where?"

I sighed. "All right, it was a fool thing to do, but I lent it to Lee. Now you see why I'm groping in the dark. If the show folds, well — maybe I get it back some day, maybe not. But Lee was in a tough spot —"

Her hand touched mine again. She said, "You're a dope, Pete. But maybe that's why I like you."

"Then you *will* marry me? That is — if Lee gets on his feet again and we get the show going O.K.? Honest, honey, I —"

And only then was I aware that somebody was standing by our table. I looked up and it was Ralph Chapman, and then I saw something else down at table level and it was the top of Colonel Toots' head.

Ralph said, "Got any idea which way we should head to find rooms?"

It took me seconds to figure out what he was talking about and get my mind on it.

"There's a hotel along the car line that goes by the lot. About ten or twelve blocks toward town. It's the nearest you can get put up at tonight, I guess. It's too late to go looking for rooms in houses."

Ralph said, "We'll go there for tonight then. They run owls on that line?"

I looked to see if Stella had finished her coffee and doughnuts, and she had. I said, "I'll borrow Lee's car and drive you guys to the hotel. Want to come along for the ride, Stella?"

She shook her head. "I'm tired, Pete. Didn't sleep much last night. I'll turn in."

"Come on then. I'll walk you back to the sleeper."

"Take your time," Ralph said. "We'll have something to eat while we're waiting for you."

Walking back along the darkened midway, I tried to bring the conversation back to the point at which it had been interrupted. But the mood was lost and I gave up. We parted amicably, but unromantically.

I knocked on the window of Lee's trailer, told him I was taking the car, and then drove it off the lot and parked it on the side nearest the chow top.

When I went back in, Gus had joined Ralph and the colonel at the table.

I said, "Hi, Gus. Don't tell me you're moving off the lot, too?"

He grinned. "If I was with your show, damned if I wouldn't. I don't blame these mugs a bit." I saw there wasn't any humor in his grin. "Pete, why don't you be smart and play safe?"

"You answered it," I told him. "I'm not smart."

Ralph was just starting a sandwich, so I sat down and called over to Hank to bring me some more coffee.

Ralph said, "Pete, it's none of my business, but did I overhear you saying something to Stella about your investing some money with Lee?"

Well, he'd called the shot; it was none of his business. So I passed it off by saying, "I'm thinking about it."

He persisted, "You mean buying a partnership in the show?"

"Maybe. Say, Ralph, remember your wondering about Lee owing Hryner some chicken feed?"

Ralph's eyes widened. "Does he admit it?"

"Sure he admits it; it wasn't any secret. Hryner's woman showed up tonight, and Lee's going to give it to her. Gave her a job, too."

"Hryner's woman? You mean that dizzy blonde Shorty was tossing steel at?" Ralph whistled. "She's three-alarm. What was a canvasman like Al doing with a doll like that?"

"Same as you'd like to do," I told him. "Hurry up that sandwich. I want to get to bed some time tonight."

It was a full hour later, though, when I put Lee's car back by the trailer and headed for the railroad car my bunk was in.

Slim Norris was coming down the steps of the car, and there was a suitcase in his hand. He lurched as his foot hit the cinder path along the rails, and I saw he was drunk.

I said, "Where you going, Slim?"

"Quitting. Hell with it." He backed along the side of the car as I stepped toward him. "Keep away from me, Gaynor."

"Slim, you're tight. Lee know you're walking out on him?"

Without thinking about it, I'd taken another step toward him, and he scuttled away backward, keeping his balance by bracing one hand against the car. "Keep away from me, Gaynor. I'll—"

Then he stepped into a patch of moonlight and I saw his eyes. They were wide with terror. He was afraid, deathly afraid—and of me. It took me a minute to get it.

Then I remembered what he'd said this morning—*had* it been only this morning?—when he'd found Bugs' body. "—murdered just like you thought'd be funny!" Because of that ill-timed wise-crack about pinning down a pincushion, Slim thought *I* was the murderer.

I said, "Dammit, Slim —" and then realized that nothing I could say would be able to convince him here and now. Particularly when I was here alone with him in the dark.

I took a step back away from him knowing that would do more good at the moment than anything I could say. Then, with my hands carefully at my sides and keeping my voice calm and low, I tried to reason with him.

I said, "Listen, Slim, Chapman and the colonel are scared to sleep on the lot, too. But they aren't running out on the show. They took rooms at the Burgoyne Hotel, Twenty-first and Hop-kins. I just drove them there. You won't be able to get a train out tonight anyway, so why don't you take a room there, too? Then think it over in the morning."

He said, "Well — yeah, but —"

"You're afraid of me because of that remark I happened to make about a pincushion last night. Did you tell the police about it?"

He shook his head.

"All right, in the morning you tell them and get it off your mind. Then you'll feel better about it."

I pointed. "See that light over there? It's an all-night drugstore. You go there and phone for a cab to take you to the Burgoyne. If you still feel the same way in the morning then tell Lee you're leaving and quit like a man."

I saw he was wavering and had sense enough not to press my advantage. Instead, I left him standing there and went on inside the car. I didn't even look out the window to see whether he was taking my advice. It wouldn't matter too much if he didn't; Lee could always get somebody else to take tickets. Just the same it would be setting a bad example. Like starting a run on a bank.

I turned on the dim light and started to undress.

If I'd turned out that light before I threw back the thin blanket to get into bed I'd never have seen it. But I didn't turn out the light because — well, I don't know just why I varied from routine that night unless subconsciously I remembered Ralph Chapman's bedroll and the toy snake that had been in it.

Anyway, I peeled back the covers, standing there dressed only in my shorts. And lying flat in the middle of my bed was a thin and flexible, but very dangerous-looking double-edged razor blade.

Chapter VIII: Under the Top

I picked the thing up, very gingerly, and then, because I don't like even to hold one of the things, I dropped it onto the window ledge. I stood looking at it with some of the feeling Ralph Chapman must have had when he looked at that toy snake.

The blade wasn't mine, of course. Needless to say, I shave with an electric razor. A nick from an ordinary razor wouldn't be fatal, in my case; I'd certainly know about it and I've got stuff that will stop the bleeding with a bit of trouble.

The blade wasn't mine, and there was no way it could have got there accidentally. It was put there either to scare me, or to kill me. I weighed the odds on which — and there was only one answer. The person who put it there couldn't have known whether it would have killed me or not. The odds were against it, but it was a definite possibility.

A cut from a really sharp blade can be painful — or the pain can be so slight as to be almost unnoticeable. I toss about a bit in my sleep, and with that blade under me I *could* have cut myself on it without feeling enough pain to awaken me, and bled to death in my sleep. Could have, yes, but it wasn't any sure-fire murder method. I might not have cut myself at all, or the cut might have been one which would have awakened me.

Slowly, I put my shirt back on, and then sat down on the edge of the bed and began to pull on my socks and shoes. I wasn't sleepy any more.

This was hitting close to home now and I had a sudden yen to talk to the police. To Helsing, if I could find him, or to Seton if I couldn't find Helsing. It takes quite a scare to make a carney feel that the coppers are his friends instead of his natural enemies, but right now I felt that way, plenty.

I was through groping in the dark on my own. I saw now that I should have insisted that Ralph go to the police about finding that toy snake. And the minute Hryner's wife had shown up on the lot I should have phoned the police and told them about it — instead of waiting to mention it casually the next time Seton came to the lot.

I should even have told them about Ralph's suspicions of Lee — even though those suspicions had turned out since to be unfounded. Loyalty to Lee was important, but it was more important to stop further murders from being committed. The police should be given all the leads, even if they were false ones. And even false ones were damned few. The further things went, the further I was from making even an intelligent guess as to who was trying to accomplish what.

It had to be one of us, I realized. Someone who knew the freak show well enough to know Bugs sometimes slept in the cooch blow, that Ralph had a morbid horror of snakes, that I had hemophilia.

I left the blade where it was and flicked out the light and left the car. I was going straight down the tracks to the street and from there to the all-night drugstore where I could phone the police.

Sure, my intentions were good. I was through messing with the case on my own — or I thought I was until I stepped down from the car.

And then I didn't move, because I heard the crunch of cinders that meant somebody walking along or across the tracks. I froze, and strained my eyes through the dimness. The footsteps were stealthy; whoever was walking was trying to do so without making any sound. Only the utter stillness of the night defeated that purpose.

Then I saw him — or her — going past the far end of the car I'd just left. A dim white figure — I could make out no details. And as soon as it stepped from the tracks to the path onto the lot, the sound of footsteps ceased.

I hesitated only an instant before I followed. True, I might be following someone on his way to the doniker — but from the attempted stealth of the footsteps, I didn't think so.

And again, I *might* be following the murderer. I might have a chance, a chance that would never come again, to find out what this was all about, possibly to avert a crime and save a life. At the very least I was going to ascertain the identity of that vague white figure.

One long step carried me to the turf along the edge of the cinders, and I ran silently along it to the path into the lot. The path turned through some trees that separated the lot from the tracks. I rounded that turn breathlessly — and just in time to see the white figure ducking under the canvas side wall of the freak-show top. A second later and I'd have been too late.

I ran up to the canvas but I didn't lift it to go under. Anyone inside would have found it too easy to see or hear that. Instead I went flat and crawled partly under.

I lay there with my head inside the tent, wondering whether I was stymied. Because I couldn't see a thing in the deeper blackness inside the top. There wasn't even enough light for me to make out the white figure if it was there.

It might even have gone on through and out the opposite side wall — but no, that was silly. Its purpose must be here inside the top, or it would have been easier to go around the freak show rather than to grope through the cluttered blackness inside.

Then, only a few yards away from me, a light shone dimly. It was a masked flashlight, but I could make out that it was held by a woman, and that the woman was Dotty Hryner.

I wriggled backward so that as little of me as possible — besides my eyes — would show, and I watched wonderingly to find out what she was doing here.

She was standing there doing nothing for the moment except flashing the dimmed light on the mitt camp. I got a side view of her as she stood that way, and of the flashlight. I could see that she had tied several thicknesses of handkerchief across the lens to dim it down — obviously so that the light wouldn't show through the tent, and so no one outside could see that a light was being used.

Yes, that much was obvious, but why she should be interested in the mitt camp was something else again. The little cubical tent of bright-red canvas where Hassan Bey told fortunes had been pitched before we'd learned that the Wilmot police wouldn't let him work. We'd let it stand because it took up space and made the interior look better. But it hadn't been used all week.

The flaps were open, as they always were except when Hassan had a mark inside.

Dotty Hryner went around the outside of the little red canvas tent first, examining and touching everything with minute curiosity. Then she examined the tent from the inside, looking along the seams, and even studying the poles. The two chairs inside were examined carefully, turned upside down, and the seats prodded. Then the little table and the stand for the mad ball.

I watched with increasing, rather than lessening bewilderment. What possible connection could there be between Dotty Hryner — if she *was* Dotty Hryner — and Hassan Bey's mitt camp. Hassan hadn't been with the show this week at all. And Dotty had just —

She must have spent all of fifteen or twenty minutes searching that crimson tent and its contents, and then she moved on, standing now before the platform on which Colonel Toots did his act. She took the bally cloth first, giving it a careful examination all the way around, feeling the seams and the fringe.

Then the diminutive chair on the platform, and—

Then I began to get it, partly. She wasn't interested, particularly in Hassan's mitt camp. She'd merely *started* there; she was making the rounds, intending to examine every bit of equipment in the top in equal detail. But for what? Had Al hidden something and told her about it in that letter of which she'd shown us only the first page? Something that may have been the motive for the crimes of the past week?

The more I thought about that the more possible it looked. It was strange that Dotty should have thrown away all of that letter except the first page, and still have kept the envelope. She hadn't shown us all the letter because the second page, the part that had the signature, also contained something she didn't want us to know.

I had an idea.

I wriggled cautiously backward until my head was safely out from under the side wall, and then I looked at my wrist watch's luminous dial. It wouldn't start to get light for a couple of hours yet. And Dotty—from the thorough manner of her search—was probably intending to spend that much time inside the top. Matter of fact, at the rate she was going, it would take her several nights to complete her search. That was undoubtedly the reason she'd been willing to take any kind of a job at any kind of wages to stay on.

I walked quietly until I was out of hearing, and then broke into a run, heading for the sleeping car—the one beyond mine—in which Stella slept. It could have been that Dotty Hryner had started her nocturnal jaunt from that very car, and if so, a spot of counter espionage would be a cinch.

I rapped quietly on Stella's window. Just loud enough, I hoped, to awaken her and no one else. After a moment the window slid up a few inches.

"Pete, what on earth do you mean by—"

"Sh-h-h, this is important. This Dotty Hryner—where's she bunking?"

"Right here in the car. Last berth down at the end. Why?"

I told her quickly where Dotty was now and what she was doing. "Can you take a look among her things without waking anyone else? Have you a flashlight?"

"Of course, but—"

"Do it, like a good egg. Maybe we can crack this thing— tonight. What you're looking for is the rest of that letter, the first page of which she showed to me and Lee. I'm going back to watch her; I'll be lying looking under the side wall. If she starts to leave there, I'll run back here ahead of her and whistle a warning."

"If I find it?"

"Bring it to me. I can't guess what to do about it till we see what it is."

She hesitated only a moment. "All right, Pete; we're fools for not calling the police instead, but—I'll do it." The window slid down again.

When I got back and looked under the side wall again, Dotty was still working on the colonel's platform. Yes, she was doing as thorough a job of it as was humanly possible without leaving signs of the search behind her.

She was just leaving that platform and starting toward the next, when there was a light touch on my back. I pulled my head out from under the side wall. It was Stella, and she had a folded paper in her hand.

She whispered, "Is this it? It's signed 'Tommy' instead of 'Al,' but it's the only part of a letter there."

I took it from her, noticing it was the same size and kind of paper as the first page of the letter Dotty had shown to Lee and me.

Stella had a flashlight in her hand and turned it on the letter as I unfolded it. It was the same handwriting as the page I had seen and followed right after it, obviously. It read:

> We'll go south. By then it'll be safe.
>
> The stuff, you know what, is hid with the show here, in a swell place. I won't say where on account of where you're staying now. Later, when you're out of that joint, I'll tell you more about it. But nothing's going to happen anyway, Babe. This is a swell set-up and I'm having fun being back with a carney for a while.
>
> Lots of love.   Tommy

I whistled softly. Things were beginning, just faintly, to make sense. Al Hryner, whose name didn't seem to be that at all, had hidden something valuable, and that must be what all the excitement was about. At any rate it was what Dotty was hunting for in there now.

Stella whispered, "That letter might be important, Pete. We better go call the police, and—"

I said, "But what if she *finds it?* She'll scram out while we're gone, and maybe we never will find out what it was. Let's wait till she goes back to the car, and—"

I lay down again quickly and stuck my head under the side wall.

Blackness. The flashlight wasn't there any more. Had Dotty heard us and left? But she couldn't have gone back the way she'd come without us seeing her. Or had she found what she was looking for—right while we were reading about it?

Well, if she'd found what she was looking for, it was my guess she'd have left quickly and without putting things back neatly, as she'd been doing on the rest of her search. Stella's flashlight would show, then, whether the search had been successful.

I took Stella's arm with one hand and lifted the side wall with the other, and we went under together. I said, "Give me the —"

And then the beam of Dotty's dimmed flashlight bracketed us. Dotty Hryner was standing behind it with a gun aimed at us. It was a tiny gun, a little .25-caliber, vest-pocket automatic, nickel-plated and with pearl handle. But it was deadly at that range. She was standing right in front of us and I cursed my stupidity for not guessing that she had heard our whispered conference outside and had come over to listen.

There was sullen anger in her face, and fear. It was the fear that frightened me a bit and made me careful. Whatever her game, she had nothing to gain by shooting us; the sound of the shots would bring people running, and it was doubtful if she'd get away. But if she was scared enough she might shoot anyway.

I tried to keep my voice calm and quiet. Rather banally, I said, "Hello, Dotty."

Her voice was shrill and ugly. "Keep your hands up. Damn you, why'd you have to butt in? You —"

"Sh-h-h," I said, "you'll wake the elephant on the other side of the lot. Listen —" And I thought fast to think what I could give her to listen to that would keep her trigger finger from getting too nervous. I got it. "Listen, suppose I could tell you where Al — Tommy — hid the stuff?"

"Take me for a sap?" Her voice oozed with scorn. "You'd have lammed with it yourself. That or turned it over for the reward, if *you* were fool enough to do that."

"I couldn't, Dotty. Come on, I'll show you why."

"Come on where?" She was wavering because I'd put conviction in my voice. The conviction that made me a good side-show barker. I was telling myself, "Forget this is a gangster's moll; she's just another mark. She'll fall for anything you tell her, like the rest of them."

I said, "In the next top." And I hoped she didn't know what the next top was; if she'd taken in the show there on her way back along the midway, then she'd be ready for the shock I was going to try on her, and my idea would be strictly no dice. Even as a give-away.

She said, "Turn around. Clasp your hands back of your head, both of you. And walk slow. I'll be behind you and you won't know which one of you this heater's aiming at."

I said, "O.K., Dotty," and followed orders very exactly. So did Stella. I noticed she still had the flashlight in her hand, but that the letter was out of sight; probably she'd stuffed it into a pocket.

We walked that way the length of the freak-show top, Dotty's flashlight behind us dimly illuminating the way. At the side wall, she said, "Wait," came up alongside and lifted the side wall high, standing halfway in and halfway out so we'd have no chance for a break as we went through. That Dotty had taken lessons somewhere; she knew her stuff. And if my hunch was right, she *would* know it.

We went under the side wall of the waxworks tent the same way, and up the aisle between the exhibits. I stopped and said, "Right here. Don't get excited, Dotty. I'm going to take Stella's flashlight so I can show you."

And, without giving her a chance to protest I reached carefully for the flash in Stella's hand, aimed it at a figure that was standing there just the other side of the ropes. A dim, shadowy, unrecognizable figure — until with startling suddenness it leaped into brilliant light as the beam of Stella's flashlight, in my hand, shone full into its realistic, if waxen, face.

And Dotty screamed. *"Tommy!"*

Chapter IX: The End of the Night

And by that time I had her by the wrist of the hand that held the gun. I twisted and she dropped it without pulling the trigger. But she turned on me with the other hand, clawing like a cat, and kicking at my ankles. But the kicks were ineffective because she was wearing soft slippers, and a moment later I had her other hand pinioned, too.

A voice behind me said quietly, "Nice work, Pete."

It was Helsing. His flashlight went on, and Dotty quit struggling.

Helsing said, "I was in the other tent, watching her. I've been spending every night there. When you butted in I thought you were going to spoil things, but —"

"But my hunch worked," I said. "Al Hryner was Tommy Benno, hiding out here after his last big job — the Eltinge bank. He wrote his moll he was using this as a hide-out — probably because he used to be a carney before he turned gunman. And somewhere here he hid the Eltinge loot — nearly half a million bucks!"

I heard Stella gasp incredulously. She was looking at the wax-works figure I had used to frighten Dotty. "But, Pete — *that* doesn't look like Al Hryner. Al's nose was different, and —"

"Plastic surgery," I told her. "On the first page of that letter to Dotty, he said, 'Doc B did a swell job.' But, of course, Dotty hadn't seen that job. She remembered him as he was, and seeing him standing there, as it were, startled her and gave me my chance to get her gun. She probably thought for a second he was still alive."

Helsing stepped forward and pocketed the gun Dotty had dropped, then slipped handcuffs on her.

He said, "Well, I guess this washes up — *the hell it does!*"

There was sudden consternation on his face as he realized, as I, too, was realizing, that it couldn't have been Tommy Benno's woman who had murdered Tommy—or Al—and Bugs Cartier, and who had—

For a moment we looked at one another blankly.

He said, "Dotty here just came into this. Somebody else—one of your mob—found out who Al Hryner was. And killed him and—Hell, it still doesn't make sense, all of it. And who—"

Suddenly it hit me. I knew who it was! There was, with the carney, only one person who could have recognized Tommy Benno in Al Hryner, despite the changed shape of his nose. There was one person with the carney who had *studied* Tommy Benno, studied and analyzed every existing photo and description. Who'd studied the shape of his hands, his chin, his ears, *all* of his physical attributes, in order to duplicate them in wax with the scrupulous accuracy Gus used on each of his wax figures. A change in the shape of the nose might fool even people who knew a man intimately, but it *wouldn't* fool a man who'd made the detailed, feature by feature study that Gus had made. Plastic surgery might fool him at first, but not for long.

I didn't realize I'd said the name out loud, until Helsing said, "Why?" and I was explaining why.

Helsing asked, "But how would he have known that Benno—Al—hid the loot with the freak show? He must have known because he must have been hunting for it the night you ran into him there and got hit."

I said, "Maybe he saw that letter, or part of it. If he'd recognized Benno he'd have been watching him. Or maybe he read Dotty's *answer* to that letter. That would have been easy; Gus acts as mailman for this end of the midway, the four shows. Front office gives him the mail and he hands it around.

"But the end of the season was coming up, and he hadn't found the money. Maybe that's why he knocked off Al, or maybe Al found him hunting for it. And Bugs, sleeping in the freak-show top, must have seen Gus searching in there. Bugs couldn't have tied it in with the murder, or he wouldn't have been bribed off with a few bucks to get drunk on. But Gus knew the police would make sense of it, if Bugs told, so he played safe by killing Bugs while he was drunk."

"But why in such a goofy way, Pete?" Helsing asked. "With the pins, I mean. And what about the snake in Bugs' bedroll?"

"That's another thing proves Gus Smith did it. He'd given up any real hope of finding it while the carney was running. But he lent money to Lee and took a lien on the props of the freak show. See it? Over the winter, they'd be his, and he'd be able to take 'em apart and put 'em together at leisure, and he was sure half a million bucks was hidden in one of them somewhere.

"If Lee paid him back he wouldn't have that chance. So if he could make Lee lose other of his acts — by scaring hell out of them, he could keep Lee from getting off the nut the rest of the season. He swiped the snake to put in Ralph's bedroll — and killed it so it would stay there. But he missed and got it in the wrong roll. Bugs was so drunk he didn't find it. And when Gus found he'd missed, he put a toy snake in Ralph's bedding — and it worked darn near as well. A few more gay little touches like that and there wouldn't have been any performers left for Lee to work with.

"And I know now why he tried to kill me, or scare me out, tonight. Because he learned I was lending money to Lee."

I heard Stella draw in her breath quickly. "He tried to kill *you*, Pete? How?"

I looked at her and I was suddenly glad — because of what I read in her face — that Gus *had* tried to kill me. It was worth it to learn what Stella's eyes told me. I said, "I'll tell you later, honey. Listen, while you're looking at me that way is the time to ask again. Will you marry me?"

Helsing snorted. "This is a hell of a time and place to —"

"Shut up," I said. "Will you, Stella?"

Stella smiled. "Not tonight, Pete. End of the season — maybe." I started to make a grab for her and remembered Helsing was there.

He cleared his throat. "Now that *that's* settled," he said dryly, "where does Gus sleep?"

But Gus was gone when we went under the partition, and I cussed myself—with Helsing's enthusiastic help—for not remembering that he was within earshot of us if he'd wakened up and listened. And very obviously he had. Just how soon he'd awakened or at what point in our conversation he'd taken French leave, we didn't know. But he was gone all right.

And then, rather quickly, it was dawn and the freak-show top was lousy with coppers again.

Lee was tearing what little was left of his hair, trying to keep them from completely demolishing the top and the props.

He glared at me. "Damn you, Pete— Yeah, they're going to pay for anything they ruin, but how can we get opened again if they make mince meat out of everything? This is worse than a blow-down!"

Seton had been using the telephone in the front office. He came over to us. "They got Gus," he told us. "Took him off a train in Springfield. But he didn't have the Eltinge bank money with him, so it's still here. We got to keep looking for it until we come across the hiding place."

Lee reached for another handful of hair.

I said, "I know where it is—maybe."

Lee grabbed at me from one side and Seton from the other, and talked at once, telling me to hurry up and say where.

I said, "If I'm right, you guys are making the same mistake Gus and Dotty made. Al's letter said it was hidden with the show, and you thought he meant the freak show. He might have meant anywhere in the carney."

Seton let go of me, and so did Lee. Seton groaned. "You mean we're going to have to take apart everything on this whole damn lot?"

"Maybe not," I told him. "Maybe that makes it easier instead of harder."

Lee echoed Seton's groan. "Look-it," he said. "They're taking the head off the bass drum, and you stand there being coy. Where the hell do you think it might be?"

I said, "Put yourself in Tommy Benno's place, *with this particular carney,* and nobody knowing who you were. What would occur to you as the cleverest place to hide something—even though nobody'd ever appreciate how clever you were?"

Seton stared at me a minute and then said, "I'll be damned," and ducked out under the side wall.

Lee looked at me blankly. "I don't get it. Where?"

I grinned. "Inside the wax effigy of himself. Seton'll know in a minute. Sh-h-h—"

A yell from the next tent told me I'd hit the jackpot.

So they quit tearing down Lee's show and we worked like the devil getting it ready to open. And by early afternoon we were ready.

Everybody in the carney was feeling much better now. We had all gone through plenty with the tension and fear that had been working on us.

And just when the crowds started to come in—it started to rain again!

FUGITIVE IMPOSTER

Dead bodies are just clay and you get used to being around them after a while and it doesn't bother you. But they aren't much in the way of company, no matter how used to them you get. That's why the night shift at an undertaker's place is just about the loneliest job there is.

By one o'clock I'd finished all the work there was to do. Cleaned and swept the place and polished the arterial tubes and trocars and what not, and uncrated the two new coffins that had come in.

And all that that left me to do was to sit down and wish I had someone to talk to that could talk back, and wish that the last three months of my apprenticeship were over so I could get my assistant's license.

And, as usual for that time of night, I was getting sleepier and sleepier, and wondering why people didn't have the consideration to do their dying always in the daytime, so there wouldn't have to be a night watch. . . .

The bell rang.

I jumped and my eyes jerked open, and I noticed first that the clock had moved ahead half an hour in the last minute. So I must have dozed off. As I headed for the door, I buttoned my coat and straightened my tie. Undoubtedly it was a customer, and when you're going to be an undertaker you've got to learn to look dignified in front of the customers — the live ones, I mean.

The instant I unlatched the door and opened it, a guy stepped through and jabbed a gun in my ribs. Then he looked me over and grinned a nasty grin and put the gun back in his pocket. I guess he decided he wouldn't need it to handle me — and I guess he was right about that.

He was a big bruiser, a head taller than I and with shoulders like a gorilla. He had cauliflower ears with hair growing out of them. And he had little, vacant-looking eyes. Just by looking at him you could see that he might be able to do dirt to a grizzly bear, but never to an equation in algebra. Obviously he was an ex-pug. And if I'd never understood what being punch-drunk meant, I understood it when I looked at him.

He reached back of him and pushed the door shut, and said in a hoarse, raspy voice: "Open the door, fat boy."

I took a step back, maybe two steps, and gawked at him. How could I open the door, when he had just — His face started to get ugly, and he pulled back a huge fist.

"B-but you just sh-shut it!" I stammered, retreating another step. That cocked fist looked as big as a barn. I knew if it hit me I'd land so hard I'd bounce.

He relaxed a little. "Not that door. The car door," he growled. "Get going."

Mine was not to reason why, just then. Keeping a watch out of the corner of my eye on Cauliflower Ears, I edged to the door of the reception room and started back for the garage doors. He stayed right with me.

I pressed the button and the doors slid silently open. A big gray sedan came through them and gunned down the ramp to a point where it was out of sight of the doors.

"Shut 'em again," said Cauliflower Ears. As I pressed the switch, the doors slid back into place.

I heard the door of the gray sedan open and slam shut, and a tall slim man, well-dressed almost to the point of foppishness, came walking up the ramp.

I recognized him right away from the pictures the newspapers had been carrying. His face was just as smoothly handsome as the photographs had shown it. But the pictures hadn't shown the character of the eyes set in that handsome face. They were fisheyes—and the eyes of a dead fish at that. Cold and gray and utterly expressionless.

The man walking up the ramp was Duke Hall. Bank robber. Cop-killer. The man who had killed five men and one woman in the course of half a dozen bank robberies within the past two years, who'd shot his way out of an ambuscade last week in Michigan, leaving one policeman dead and two others wounded behind him.

Duke Hall, who had bragged he could hit any given button of a policeman's coat at fifty feet, but that he never aimed at a button high up because the cop would die too easily. Duke Hall, the most wanted, feared and hated criminal in the country.

Duke Hall, here in Fenimore Brothers' Funeral Parlors! I didn't know what it was all about, and I couldn't even guess. But I felt myself getting cold all over, starting at the base of my spine and working up and down from there.

He was looking at the gorilla standing beside me. "Is Pudgy here the only guy around, Punchy?" he asked. His voice was as cold and gray as his eyes.

The gorilla started to grin. "Funny, Duke," he answered. "He's Pudgy and ya call me Punchy. Pudgy and Punchy." He broke into a hoarse guffaw.

The killer's voice cut like a whip. "Case this joint, you half-witted ape! How do you know he's alone here?" He took a step toward the ex-pug and there was death in his face.

Punchy whirled, his face white as a sheet, and headed back

for the parlors. But humor overcame his fear; I heard him chuckling to himself before he got to the first door. He walked oddly — came down hard on his heel with each step, and then lifted his foot without any spring to it, like someone on stilts.

Then my eyes came back to Duke Hall and I saw he was looking at me. I didn't like the look.

"Pudgy," he said, "we want to buy some meat."

I don't know whether it was what he said or the way he said it or the way he looked. But I didn't answer. Because I couldn't.

"About a hundred and fifty pounds of it, Pudgy. Five or ten pounds one way or the other is all right. We want it in a cut about five feet eleven inches long. Cold meat will do."

"Y-you mean you w-want —" I stammered.

"You look like a very smart guy, Pudgy. You get the idea right away. That's what I want. A stiff. Only better if it isn't stiff yet. See what I mean, Pudgy?"

He leaned back against the fender of Fenimore Brothers' best touring car, and lighted a cigarette. He watched me over the flare of the match. Ice over flame.

The big guy showed up again in the doorway. There was a lopsided grin on his face. "Lots of people here, Duke," he said. "But they won't bother us none. They're all croaked." He guffawed again.

Duke's glance flicked toward him and he stopped in the middle of a laugh.

"Take us to the office, Pudgy," Duke told me. "Or some room without outside windows. You look like a smart guy and that's to the good if you don't try to be too smart. You can do more good if you know just what I want and what I want it for. Can't you?"

I managed to unlimber my neck enough to nod, even if I didn't know what he meant. Then I led the way toward Mr. Fenimore's office. My legs felt like they were made of rubber.

I fell into a chair, and Duke Hall sat on the edge of the desk, not facing me. I was glad of that. Cauliflower Ears leaned against the closed door.

"Look, kid," said Duke Hall. "You know who I am, don't you?"

"Uh — yes."

"They know I'm here in Elkhorn." He didn't have to explain who "they" were — I knew, of course, he meant the cops. "There's a cordon around the town. A dozen of 'em bunched together on every road out. And I've got to get through tonight."

His voice was as flat and expressionless as though he were talking about the weather.

"They know my car. I could get another, but they're stopping all cars. See?"

I saw. Beyond his unemotional statement of fact, I began to get the picture. There wasn't a policeman in the country wouldn't risk his life to get the cop-killer, Duke Hall. Outside there, on the roads, they were waiting. Some openly, some in ambush.

Yes, the countryside would be hot all right, since the police knew Duke Hall was in town and suspected he was going to try to run the gauntlet. There'd be Tommy-guns waiting out there, and tear-gas bombs, and maybe even barricades. And all the state cops would be converging on Elkhorn, and even whatever Feds were near-by. Duke Hall was Big Time, with capital letters.

"They've even got lookouts in the fields," Duke went on. "There's only one way I can get through tonight, Pudgy. They're gonna find me dead, see? And open the roads again."

I began to see, a little. But how could —

"Highway 41," he went on, "is blocked at the Bender Road. A mile this side of there, there's a barn. When that barn burns down in an hour or so, they'll see the flames and some of them will investigate, see? This car that they know I'm using will be hidden near it. And there'll be a charred stiff found in the barn that will be taken for me. A couple bottles to show I got drunk hiding out in the barn, and —"

"But can't they tell that—"

He nodded. "Yeah, but they'll think so right away. When they get that stiff back to the morgue and begin to check Bertillions, sure. But that'll be tomorrow."

It looked possible. Not sure, of course, but the kind of a gambling chance a guy like Duke Hall would be willing to take. Duke was looking at me, and when I glanced across at his companion by the door, he seemed to read what I was thinking.

"Punchy's local talent," he said. "I picked him up here to help me. The cops don't know he's with me, so we won't need a stiff for him."

He stopped talking and for a full minute only the ticking of the clock filled the office. Then Duke Hall looked at me and said, "Well?" and I realized that it was my move.

I guess it was because I'd been so scared that I hadn't realized while he was talking where I'd fitted in. I had to furnish the corpse. And if I didn't or couldn't, it didn't take much figuring on my part to know where I stood with a killer like Hall.

I saw Duke signal to Punchy, and the big gorilla began to move across the room toward me.

I began to talk fast. "There's six of them in the morgue, Mr. Hall," I told him. "But I don't know. Three of them are women and that wouldn't be any good, naturally. Then there's Mr. Cordovan, but he—no, that's no good. And Mr. Rogers is a dried-up little old shrimp and I don't remember the other one's name, but he—he's a lot heavier than I am. And that's all there—"

The big gorilla was back of my chair now, and I didn't know what he was going to do. I tried to twist around to face him, but Duke Hall's gray eyes held me like a cobra's hold a bird. I'd never known until then what it meant to be scared stiff.

"How tall are you, Pudgy?" Duke asked quietly.

At first I couldn't get my throat to work. Then I swallowed. "F-five feet six," I managed to say.

I thought maybe I was getting away with it. But Duke's eyes didn't waver from mine. "You're lying, Pudgy. You're five-eight, at least. And lying down a couple or three inches isn't that much. And if it was a really good fire that didn't leave much but a skeleton of you, Pudgy, maybe —"

Almost as though I had eyes in the back of my head, I could visualize the grin on Punchy's face as he put his hands around my neck.

"Okay, Duke?" he asked. And laughed as he began to tighten his grip.

I managed to holler, "Wait!" squeakily before those tremendous hands had tightened too much to let my voice out.

I saw Duke signal, and the pressure relaxed. He looked at me and said: "Well?"

I said, "Listen —" to stall an instant.

My mind was going like mad. I didn't have an idea, but I was trying to get one. I was going to die if I didn't get one. These boys weren't playing. Maybe I'd die later no matter what I could pull out of the hat now, but that was later; this was *now*.

Maybe they'd try to use me for an understudy for the corpse they wanted, but I didn't think so. Probably they'd try another undertaking parlor or else pick up a guy off the street that fitted closer. But that didn't matter to me. They wouldn't go off and leave me alive to call copper. Unless I came through with something, I was as good as dead.

"I — I was stalling," I told him. "We got a corpse that will do." I felt Punchy take his hands away from my neck, and I went on. "He's about five-ten, and I'd guess about your build. And he hasn't any embalming fluid in him, because he's going to be cremated tomorrow. I don't know how embalming fluid would act in a fire."

"Show me, Pudgy."

My legs almost gave way under me when I got up. I took them back to the morgue and opened the gray casket that was still on the dolly.

Duke Hall stood looking down, sizing up the build and appearance of the corpse. "Swell," he said. "Same color hair and everything. Just so the face gets charred, it'll be a dead ringer." He reached down and prodded the flesh of one of the folded hands. "Rigor mortis, though."

"Probably wearing off by now," I told him. "No embalming fluid. I think fire'll break it, anyhow." I took hold of a trouser cuff and lifted a little and the leg came up. "Yeah, wearing off."

Duke turned and called over my shoulder to Punchy. "Hey, help the kid put this stiff in the car. That black touring car out there."

The gorilla was stronger than I; I had him take the shoulders and I took the feet and we got the corpse into the touring car. I saw Duke giving the car and the license plates a close once-over to be sure there was nothing that would mark it as a mortician's car.

We'd got the body doubled up in the back seat when he finished.

"Okay," he said. "Pudgy here will drive this car and I'll go with him. You, Punchy, follow us with the gray sedan. When we get there I'll show you where to park it so it'll look hidden but where the cops will find it when they go to the fire."

The streets ahead of us, and then the road, stayed empty. But Duke had me stick to thirty miles an hour so there'd be no chance of us attracting attention.

The ex-pug and I carried the body into the barn and put it on a pile of straw in the corner. Duke watched all the details. I remembered one he almost forgot.

"How about a gun?" I asked him. "They'll expect to find one on the corpse."

He reached hesitantly toward a shoulder holster, and then reconsidered. "You, Punchy," he said. "Put yours in one of the guy's pockets."

Punchy started to protest, then caught Duke's eye and grinned instead, and obeyed. Then Punchy and I waited in the touring car while Duke touched off the straw with his cigarette lighter. He came running up and got in the driver's seat beside me.

We just made it. As we turned off the main road into a hiding place for the touring car, the sky was beginning to turn red behind us and we could hear the roar of motorcycles and police cars as several of them converged toward the burning barn.

But back among the trees where we parked, the car was safely out of sight. A fire engine sirened past us, whizzing out from town.

Duke looked up at the bloody sky to the west of us, and nodded in satisfaction.

"Take 'em half an hour to put it out, and that's more than plenty of time." He leaned back against the seat and lighted another cigarette. "I'll give 'em an hour more to find me in that barn and find the car by it, and call off the cordon."

"Jeez, Duke," Punchy told him. "You're a smart guy, all right. How's about the kid, here. Do we —"

"He's smart, too," said Duke Hall. "Damn near too smart, at first. But he dug us up the right corpse, so maybe we'll give him a break. We'll let him drive us through."

He turned toward me. All the car lights were off, of course, and I couldn't see his eyes, but I could feel them. And I could remember them. I knew right then that when the getaway was finished, they'd knock me off.

If they let me out, it wouldn't be long before I could get to a telephone. Unless they fixed me so I couldn't.

In spite of what I'd done, there was still a swell chance of that happening. But you can't stay in a state of jitters forever; you get calluses. I wasn't so much afraid any more. After that moment when Punchy had those hamlike hands of his around my neck and started to squeeze, I don't think I'll be so much afraid of anything any more.

We heard the fire engine clanging back into town, and we heard other cars, too, but from where we were we couldn't tell which way they were going.

None of us talked. Duke smoked one cigarette after another.

Punchy didn't smoke. Every once in a while he'd laugh aloud, or start to, at some joke of his own. Duke would turn around and glance at him and the sound would break off abruptly.

I had plenty to think about. I wondered a little what Mr. Fenimore would say about my giving Mr. Cordovan's corpse to Duke Hall. But I guessed he wouldn't say much; I really didn't have any choice. And Mr. Cordovan had wanted to be cremated anyway, and he was getting his wish, only a few hours sooner. And as he didn't have any relatives, the only squawk could come from the crematory for the business they lost.

The sky began to turn a little gray in the east now, where we could see between the trees. Duke Hall looked at his wrist watch.

"Almost four," he said. "Let's go. You drive, Pudgy. Stay under forty till we're well out of town. I'll take over then."

I slid the car out onto the road. Now within five minutes I'd know whether my stunt had worked or not. But even if it had, I might end up with a bullet or two in me. Duke Hall held his hand near the lapel of his coat.

I tried to make up my mind what I could do if anybody tried to stop the car. If I stopped it, Duke Hall would shoot me. If I didn't, someone else would. A swell spot.

The Bender Road intersection was coming up ahead. I let the car drop to thirty. Duke turned his head to look at me, but I pretended I didn't notice.

I let the speed drop to twenty-five. Duke growled: "Hey, don't —"

Then a couple of blue-clad figures stepped onto the road ahead of us. A car that had been parked out of sight swung out onto the road and I could see a Tommy-gun muzzle ready at the back window. One of the blue-clad figures had a hand raised for us to stop. His other hand rested on the butt of the holstered gun on his belt. But the gun wasn't drawn. They didn't know yet that we weren't okay.

I heard Duke swear luridly and saw his gun leap from its holster under his coat. He brought it up to fire through the windshield. With his marksmanship, I know every shot would find a policeman target.

I pushed all my weight on the brake, suddenly and hard. Even at twenty-five miles an hour, that's a jolt. Duke went forward and the windshield broke, but it wasn't a bullet that broke it; it was the gun itself smashing through the glass.

I heard a yell from Cauliflower Ears in the back seat as he fell forward and thumped against the back of the front seat. But I knew he wasn't armed.

I'd braced myself against the steering wheel when I'd smacked the brake home, and I'd been ready for the jolt. I threw my weight sidewise against Duke and got both my hands on his arm as he was trying to raise the gun again. He clubbed at my face with his free hand and I saw stars, but hung on.

Then the car was at a dead stop and there were coppers with guns on all sides of it. One of them jumped to the running-board and yanked the gun out of Duke's hand—and it was all over.

As they pulled us out of the car I recognized Chief of Police Jerry Harrison and he recognized me and said: "Charlie! What the hell are you doing with—"

I spilled the story, and he grinned. "Charlie, you're going to get a slice of that reward! Or rather, those rewards. There are a dozen of them waiting to be claimed."

He chuckled. "So Duke thought we'd think that was him back in the barn, huh?"

I nodded. "I told him we didn't have a corpse that would do, but he was going to make me pinch-hit for one. I figured that even a body with *two artificial legs* would be better than that— from my point of view if not his."

CLIENT UNKNOWN

Carey Rix stared in surprise at the man behind the hotel desk.

"You say Room Two-o-eight is empty?" he repeated. "Are you sure?"

The clerk nodded, looking strangely at Rix.

"If you know anything about the guy that checked in here yesterday, you'd better go up," he said. "The police are up there. Something funny happened—something darned funny."

Carey Rix wanted a moment to think before going up to 208. He lighted a cigarette, turned to the clerk.

"What was the guy's name?" he asked.

"Frank. Just a moment." He leafed back to yesterday's page in the register on the desk and pointed to an entry. "F. Frank. The younger guy that was with him didn't sign. Said he wasn't staying."

Rix walked up to the second floor and along the single corridor. He passed 204 and 206. The next door was slightly ajar. On it he saw the outline, lighter than the rest of the door, of the figures 208. The brass numerals themselves had been removed.

Carey Rix tapped lightly and pushed the door open. Two detectives, one of whom he recognized as Sergeant Stanger, were standing in an empty room, an absolutely stripped room.

"Hi, Rix," said the sergeant. "Know anything about this? It's goofy."

Rix looked around. There wasn't a stick of furniture in the room. Lighter spots on the wall showed that pictures had been removed. The curtain and shade had been taken from the window. If there had been a carpet on the floor, it wasn't there now. His eyes went back to Sergeant Stanger.

"What gives, Sarge?" he asked. "Termites?"

The sergeant frowned. "Maybe it's funny to a private detective like you. But I'm supposed to make a report on this. What do you know about this F. Frank? Who was he?"

Rix shook his head in denial. "Yesterday afternoon, about five o'clock, a guy called my office. I wasn't there. Sue made an appointment for me to call at Room Two-o-eight at the Avalon at ten a.m. today. The guy didn't give a name. Well, here I am."

The sergeant looked at him narrowly.

"You wouldn't kid me, would you, Carey? When you walked in here, I thought we'd sure get a lead."

"I wouldn't kid you about this, Sarge. What's your angle? There must be a night clerk here. How could they have taken all this stuff out without his knowing it?"

Stanger spat disgustedly into a corner.

"They doped him. The young guy who came in with the old guy gave him a drink. He got sleepy and dozed off, and didn't wake up till four a.m. The drink business happened about midnight."

"There's a back door on the alley," added the other police detective. "It's only a couple of yards from here to the stairs, and the door's at the bottom. They could have cleaned this room in half an hour. But why did they do it?"

"Well, you got a case at last, Rix." Sergeant Stanger grinned suddenly. "A swell one, whatever it is. How's the new agency coming? Sorry you quit with Argus Agency."

"Nope, not yet. Business is great, Sarge, but maybe I can sandwich in time to look for my client on this one. I suppose you got a couple of descriptions. Swell. Let's have them."

He copied the descriptions of F. Frank and his younger companion from Stanger's notebook. They certainly weren't minutely detailed descriptions. The man who had registered had been described by the clerk as about sixty, medium height, slight build, had a bad cough. The younger man was taller, heavier, seemed better dressed, and looked like a professional man — a lawyer, maybe, or a doctor.

"Thanks, Sarge," Rix said when he had finished copying the notes. "If I get anything, I'll let you know as soon as possible."

Slowly he walked back to the office. Unless he got an idea somehow, there wasn't any reason for hurry. He didn't know what he could do when he got there.

Sue Moran looked up as he entered. She jerked a sheet of paper from her typewriter.

It was covered from the top to the bottom with one sentence stating that that moment was the proper time for all good men to come to the aid of a certain unnamed party.

"Don't tell me, after two months of waiting, that we've got a case, Carey?" she blurted.

"Angel, we sure have. I told you I'd land one if I stuck it out long enough. And this is just the beginning."

She opened a drawer of the desk, took out a printed form in duplicate. Inserting a carbon between the sheets, she put the form in the typewriter.

"Okay," she said. "Let's go. First blank is for the client."

Carey Rix perched on a corner of her desk and smiled down at her.

"Client: unknown," he dictated. "And here's the rest of the dope. Retaining fee: nothing. Daily rate: highly doubtful. Object of investigation: have no idea whatever. Put all that down, Angel."

She didn't. Instead, she leaned back in her chair and looked up at him with a reproachful, worried frown.

"Carey," she said soberly, "do you realize that opening this agency and keeping it open for two months has cost you nearly a thousand dollars, what with the furniture and everything? How much longer do you think you can keep on without a case?"

He reached down and ran a forefinger up across her forehead to erase the frown.

"I've got a case, Sue. Somebody whose name may have been F. Frank called on me, and I'm going to find out what he wanted. Then I'll get it for him, and send him a bill."

As he gave her a quick sketch of what had happened at the hotel, he saw her eyes widen.

"But, Carey, it doesn't make sense. The furniture in that room couldn't have been worth enough to —"

"Angel, you miss the point. The brass numerals on the door were gone, too, and the rate card that hung on the back of the door. Everything was taken, whether it was worth a shout in Sheol, or less. Now add that up. What do you get?"

"A headache," Sue answered. Then her eyes grew thoughtful. "Unless someone had a room about that size somewhere, and wanted to make it into a duplicate of the hotel room, complete with rate card and everything."

"Go to the head of the class, Angel. That's our lead! But where it gets us, I haven't any idea."

He rose and began to pace the length of the office.

At the end of the fifth trip, he stopped at Sue's desk, thumbed open the telephone directory to the classified section.

"Whoever took that stuff out," he said, "must have used a truck. The bed — even taken apart — and the dresser, wouldn't have loaded into a passenger car. Wonder how many trucking companies there are in this town."

"Plenty," Sue told him grimly. "It'd take a week to canvas half of them." She leaned across the desk, helped him find the right place. "Look at that list!"

The regular listings were among the inner columns of the

book. The outer columns carried display advertisements of the larger trucking concerns. Carey Rix put his finger on the largest display advertisement in the outer column of the right-hand page.

"Look, Angel. Timothy Trank Cartage Company."

"So what?" demanded the secretary.

"So maybe nothing. But look." Carey Rix took his notebook and pencil from his pocket. "Here's what T. Trank looks like. T. Trank is Timothy Trank. Now watch."

He drew a horizontal bar through each T. The name now read F. Frank.

"It could be," he pursued. "Or it could be an accident. But if the old guy registered as T. Trank, and any one wanted to change that registration, all he had to do was take the desk pen and make two little marks. Sue, call the Chamber of Commerce and get me what dope you can on the Timothy Trank Cartage Company."

A few minutes later, Sue put the transceiver back on its cradle, and read from the shorthand notes she had taken.

"Timothy Trank is retired. He's sixty. His son, Roger Trank, runs the business for him. Another son, John, is a doctor. John has an interest, too. It's a family business, sort of."

"Addresses?"

"Timothy Trank lives in Wyandotte, thirty miles out from town. So does his son, Dr. John Trank. Roger lives in town, at Sixteen-seventy-five Kane Place."

Carey Rix walked to the window and looked out. Sue turned and watched him. For the first time she realized what a big difference there was in her employer since he had returned from the Avalon Hotel. He had been moping around the office for two months, his face getting longer each day the agency drew a blank, his shoulders gradually sagging. Now his whole body seemed like a coiled spring. This was the Carey Rix she'd almost forgotten existed. She smiled at his eagerness as he resumed pacing the office. What did it matter if there wasn't a fee in sight?

"Call up Timothy Trank, Angel!" he snapped. "If he's there, I'll talk to him. If he isn't, find out all you can."

Timothy Trank was not at home. Sue had a bit of difficulty pumping the servant who had answered the phone, but at last she was satisfied she had all the information he could give her.

"Mr. Trank came in to town yesterday afternoon," she told Carey. "His son John drove him in. He was going to get in touch with them and tell them where he'd be staying, but he hasn't called home yet. He expected to be in the city for several days. Maybe your hunch is working. Want me to call Roger Trank?"

Carey Rix grabbed his hat and started for the door.

"Never mind, Angel. I'll go out there myself."

He slowed his car across the street and a few doors away from 1675 Kane Place. It was a two-story brick residence. As he pulled to the curb and parked, he saw the door of Roger Trank's house open.

A tall, slim man, wearing a snap-brim hat pulled down over his eyes, left the house. Rix waited until he had rounded the corner and gone out of sight before he left the car. The slim man had seemed vaguely familiar. Rix had seen him somewhere before — was it in a police lineup?

A maid in a starched uniform answered Carey's ring at the door of 1675 Kane Place.

"Is Mr. Roger Trank in?" he asked.

The maid looked him over and seemed to like what she saw, for she smiled briefly before answering.

"He's out right now. Be back shortly, sir."

"The gentleman who just left here," said Carey. "I recognized him, but I can't place him. Do you know who he is?"

"Yes, sir," replied the maid. "Would you care to come in and wait for Mr. Trank? The gentleman who left here a moment ago is Mr. Rix — Mr. Carey Rix."

"Oh," said Carey. "Yes, I've met Mr. Rix. Odd that I wasn't able to place him the minute I saw him. Yes, I'll wait for Mr. Trank."

She took his hat and showed him to the parlor.

"By the way," Rix asked as she turned to leave, "is Mr. Timothy Trank here?"

She nodded. "I think he's sleeping now. It's too bad."

"Isn't it?" Carey smiled sympathetically. "Is he—uh—completely—"

"Dr. John says there's hope if they humor him. And they certainly are, fixing up that room and all."

"I hope he's right," said Carey. "It must be a lot of trouble keeping up the pretense."

He chose a comfortable chair and sat down, facing the doorway of the room. The maid's footsteps died away to silence as she went to the back part of the house.

Carey waited until he heard her close a door behind her. Then he rose silently, tiptoed out into the hall, and up the staircase. It was heavily carpeted and his feet made no sound.

There was no mistaking the room he sought. The brass numerals "208" on the outside of the door at the end of the upstairs hallway left no doubt.

He did not doubt, either, that the door opened inward. Otherwise a man in bed in that room would not see the outside of the door when it was opened. In that case, there would be no need for the brass numerals.

He turned the knob silently, pushed the door ajar, and peered into the darkened room. The covers on the bed outlined the slight figure of an elderly man, whose gray head rested upon the pillow. He breathed heavily in deep slumber.

Carey Rix stepped quietly into the room and closed the door. The shade was pulled down at the single window of the little room, but enough light came in around it to enable him to see clearly as he looked about the room.

It was almost the same size and shape as Room 208 at the Avalon Hotel. Undoubtedly the furniture and the carpet were from the hotel room. The Avalon's rate card and instructions to guests hung from a nail on the back of the door.

To a man forbidden to arise from bed, unable to walk to the window or door to investigate his surroundings, the room was nearly a perfect imitation of the hotel room Timothy Trank had taken at the Avalon.

Quietly Rix skipped closer to the bed and looked at the sleeping man. He seemed to slumber soundly, a natural sleep, but Carey couldn't be sure of that.

As he stood there, wondering whether or not to awaken Timothy Trank, he heard a door open and close nearby. There were footsteps approaching the room of the sick man.

Rix looked about hastily. He darted to a closet and got inside just as the door of the room opened. Carey left the closet door ajar.

The tall, heavily built man who entered carried a bottle and a spoon in his left hand. He walked to the bed and put a hand on Timothy Trank's shoulder.

"Dad," he said. "Wake up. Time to take this medicine."

The old man opened his eyes with a great effort.

"Hello, John," he mumbled.

He raised himself on one elbow. His eyes drooped shut again. John Trank took the cork from the bottle, tilted it to pour some of the liquid into the spoon.

Carey Rix pushed open the door, was across the room in three quick strides. Making no effort to be silent, he got there before John Trank could turn.

"Stay where you are, Doctor!" he ordered as he jabbed a rigid forefinger against John Trank's back. "And I wouldn't give that to your patient, if I were you."

The eyes of Timothy Trank had gone wide. Carey Rix spoke to him over John's shoulder.

"I'm Carey Rix, Mr. Trank — the real Carey Rix. You've been talking to an impostor that your sons are ringing in on you. You're being made the victim of a conspiracy. Why, I don't know."

John Trank didn't turn, but he spoke angrily to the man on the bed.

"That's absurd, Dad! Whoever this man is, he's lying. I —"

Carey Rix' attention had been fixed on the events in the room. He hadn't heard the second set of footsteps approaching. When the door opened, and a middle-aged, bald man, whom he hadn't seen before, came into the room, he was caught unaware.

Carey's finger, poked into the doctor's back in lieu of a gun, would be obvious to the man who had opened the door. He dropped his hand, pivoted to face the newcomer.

"Who is this, John?" demanded the bald man. His hand dropped into his coat pocket, came out with a small nickel-plated .32 revolver. "What's he doing here?"

Carey felt his arms pinned behind him as the doctor took a sudden step toward him. He didn't dare fight with the revolver pointed at his midriff.

"I suppose you're Roger Trank," he said. "I'm Carey Rix. I want to know why you're —"

The powerful man behind propelled him forward with a vicious shove that cut off his speech in mid-sentence.

"He's some impostor, Roger," bellowed the doctor furiously. "I don't know what his game is, but we'll turn him over to the police and let them find out."

"The police," said Rix as the two men took him down the stairs, "will be just the logical answer."

"Shut up!" grated Roger Trank. Once out of hearing of the old man in the upstairs room, his manner had changed completely. "The police aren't going to be in on this. Tie him up, John. We'll decide what to do with him when Spike gets back."

Spike! Rix remembered now where he had seen the tall man,

in the snap-brim hat, who had been leaving the house when he arrived. The bogus Carey Rix was Spike Gordon, gambler and con man. Carey had seen him in many a lineup at Headquarters.

Dr. John Trank found a rope, tied Carey's arms behind him, then bound his ankles.

"In the closet!" Rogert Trank grabbed one of Carey's arms and motioned to his brother to take the other. "When Spike gets back, we'll figure out what to do with him."

Between them, the brothers carried him to the hall closet. Before Roger closed the door he spoke threateningly.

"One peep out of you, Rix, and we'll know what to do."

The door slammed and the key turned in the lock. Left alone in the darkness, Carey Rix wasted no time getting to work. He knew how his fate would have to be decided. It was decided already, for that matter. The brothers merely wanted Spike to help with the details of removing the body.

His ankles were bound, but the closet was too small for him to fall down, as long as he kept his knees and body rigid. He shifted his weight, groped behind with his hands until he found what he sought.

It was the head of a nail that was projecting from the wall, low enough so he could get at it. Though it was four feet from the floor, by bending sideward, he could reach it with his wrists. An old sweater hung on the nail. He dropped it to the floor and went to work on the knot, trying to catch the proper loop on the head of the nail.

It was slow, hard work. Frequently the ache in his arms became intolerable, forcing him to rest unwillingly. How long or short the minutes were, he had no idea. But it must have taken at least a half hour before he loosened the knot, slipped the rope over his wrists, and untied his ankles.

The lock was easy. They hadn't searched his pockets, except for a quick frisk to make sure he didn't have a gun. In his vest pocket he carried a small pick-lock with which he was able to grip the end of the key in the old-fashioned lock. He turned it silently.

He reached for the knob, then pulled his hand back. He had heard the sound of the front door opening, the clump of steps coming from the living room.

"Glad you're back, Spike," John's voice said. "Something came up. Carey Rix is here."

There was a muttered exclamation from the con man, then more footsteps, and the sound of the living room door closing.

That didn't leave Rix much time. He bent down quickly and untied his shoes. He stepped out of them, opened the door and left the closet.

As he crossed the hall and started up the stairs, he could hear the murmur of voices from the living room.

Upstairs, he turned the knob of the door marked 208. He put his fingers to his lips in an appeal for silence as he stepped into the pseudo hotel room. The sick man was awake. He looked at Carey Rix doubtfully, but he made no outcry.

Carey closed the door behind him and spoke quietly, so his voice wouldn't carry downstairs.

"I really am Carey Rix, Mr. Trank," he said. "I've got to explain things to you fast, and you've got to believe me."

He crossed to the window, pulled up the shade.

"Come here to the window, Mr. Trank, and look out. Then you'll know. You can reach it all right. You're not as sick as your son is making you believe."

Timothy Trank stared at the private detective uncertainly for a moment. Then he threw back the covers and started to cross the room. He wobbled a bit as he reached the window. Carey put a supporting arm about Trank as the old man gaped through the glass.

"Roger's house," Trank said slowly, his face going bleak and gray.

Rix helped him back into bed, then sat down on the edge of the mattress.

"What was it you wanted to see me about, Mr. Trank, when you made the original appointment?"

The old man lay back and closed his eyes as he answered.

"The business was losing money, and it shouldn't have been. I suspected Roger was taking company funds, but I wanted to know. I didn't suspect John. Yet he must have been working with Roger."

Carey nodded. "And when John found out you were going to have an investigation, he knew he and Roger were sunk unless he could sidetrack it. They would both be disinherited, maybe prosecuted, if you found out."

"I trusted John," said the old man faintly. "But Roger —"

"They doped you and brought you here. They were going to keep you in this room while a friend of Roger's impersonated me, pretending to conduct an investigation. Of course, he'd report to you that everything was okay. Then you'd be satisfied, so they planned to dope you again and take you home. They'd tell you that you were taken there while you were in a coma. After that, John would let you get well again — or maybe he wouldn't."

"I think he would," the old man answered. "The bulk of my estate goes to charity. Apparently my sons are raiding the business while they have control of it, while I'm still alive. I'd be worth less to them if I were dead."

Most of Carey Rix' thoughts were on his conversation with Timothy Trank. But a part of his mind had been listening for sounds downstairs, and he heard them now.

A door opened. There were footsteps in the hallway. He heard low-pitched conversation as the three men reached the bottom of the staircase. Then there was the sound of their footsteps as they started to ascend.

There wasn't a second to waste, or he'd be trapped. He raced through the door of Timothy Trank's room and was sprinting down the hall before they reached the landing. His shoeless feet made no sound.

He paused briefly just around the corner from the top of the staircase, waited until he judged the first was half a dozen steps from the top. Now was the time! The advantage of position and surprise should balance the three-to-one odds against him.

He leaped around the corner, left the floor in a headlong diving tackle that caught John Trank around the waist. The doctor was carried over backward, crashing into the two men behind him.

The stair landing shook with the impact. Carey Rix scrambled off the top of the heap, knew he was unhurt.

He swung his fist into the face of Roger Trank. The bald-headed man had partly risen and was reaching for the revolver in his pocket.

Spike Gordon, Carey's impersonator, was out cold. His head had struck the wall as he'd been carried backward. John was still prone, staring around dazedly.

Roger's head snapped back under the force of Rix' blow, but his hand came up from his pocket with the revolver. Carey's foot lashed out. It struck Roger Trank's wrist as the gun roared. The bullet buried itself in the wall behind Carey.

He lunged forward, caught Roger's wrist with both hands, and twisted. The revolver fell. Carey leaped, scooped it up.

"Are you all right, Mr. Rix?" he called.

Carey looked up. Old Timothy Trank, in his nightgown, stood at the top of the stairs. He held the bannister for support. He seemed to have aged five years since Carey Rix had revealed the conspiracy against him. Carey took a few backward steps toward him.

"It's all over, Mr. Trank. Shall I phone the police?"

The old man's face was gray as the hair above it as he looked down at the trio on the landing. Two of them were his sons. They had conspired to rob him, and would not have stopped at murder to serve their ends.

"Yes, Mr. Rix," he replied slowly. "You may call the police."

He swayed and would have fallen, if Carey Rix had not caught him.

It was a week later, in Carey Rix' office, that Sue Moran had held up the envelope as Carey came in.

"This is it!" she exulted. "Timothy Trank's return address is on the envelope. Shall I open it, or do you want the fun?"

"Go ahead, Angel," he said in a martyred voice.

Eagerly she ripped open the envelope, snatched out a piece of paper that looked exactly like a check.

"One thousand bucks! That pays for the furniture, all expenses, our salaries, and actually puts us a little ahead!"

Carey sat down thoughtfully on the corner of her desk.

"How much ahead?" he asked sternly.

She made a hasty mental computation. "About sixty-five dollars," she said at last.

Rix smiled at her, and his voice was half serious, half kidding as he said:

"Angel, the way I feel right now, I don't ever want to be rich. A man with money can't trust anyone, not even his own family. So tonight you are going to put on your fanciest gingham apron, and I'll call for you at nine. We'll see how many night clubs will help us get rid of that surplus sixty-five smackers."